Sheila Pain

The Fabric of Her Life

by
Sheila Painter

Printed in the United States of America

First Printing, 2018

ISBN: 9781731535016

Preface

This book is a work of fiction. Those who know me might swear it is autobiographical. But although there is much overlap with my life, I can assure you, this book is not about me. Any resemblance to persons living or dead is purely coincidental. Unless it's not.

~Sheila Painter

BLOG: Therefore I Quilt

Get some inspiration!

Posted: Nov 1, 2017 05:48 PM EDT

Here's a little nugget for you, quilters! Poet Marvin Bell said, "Much of our lives involves the word 'no.' In school we are mostly told, 'Don't do it this way. Do it that way.' But art is the big yes. In art, you get a chance to make something where there was nothing." If we substitute the word 'quilting' for the word 'art', this applies to what we do, right?!?

We cut up beautiful fabric and sew it back together into something wonderful. It's a bit like magic. It's definitely art. And it's my honor to share this art with you.

Many people have said that seeing quilts and quilt tops displayed gets their creative juices flowing. Stop in to a quilt shop and be inspired. Attend a quilt show. Read quilt magazines and books. Join a quilt guild and pay close attention during show 'n tell. I promise, you'll find a treasure you haven't seen before, and you WILL be inspired. Then you'll have "a chance to make something where there was nothing."

And on a personal note, thank you everyone, for bearing with me over this last very stressful year. I'm soldiering on, and back to my normal routine. That is, the new normal. I appreciate each and every warm and caring comment from you, my blog readers. I pledge to get back to regular blog posts from now on, because, remember: Therefore I Quilt! ~Ann

How are you holding up, Ann?

Not bad. I'm not crying every day, so that's a plus.

I'm glad to hear it. I hope our phone conversations have helped. Do you think you're ready to get back in the swing of things?

I think yes, but it's hard.

I completely understand. Don't forget, you're sorta RSVPd for that charity event tomorrow night. It's a good way to honor Pete.

I remember. It's on my calendar. But after all these months, it still feels like yesterday. I don't know if I can do this.

Life goes on. You've gotta keep going.

Believe me, Debby, I know that. I just can't decide about this fundraiser thing. I have to get dressed up!

I'd sure love to see you!

I miss everyone. But should I? I can't decide.

I'll decide for you. Cocktails at 6:30, dinner at 7. Bring your checkbook. Be there.

OK, See U tomorrow. (gulp)

The posh banquet room was a riot of balloons, flowers and shiny stuff, and Kevin squinted as he entered. He was glad he wasn't on the decorations committee; he'd have hated inflating balloons and taping mylar on walls. His invitations job was much simpler, and best of all, done. He hadn't even had to lift a finger, as he had his office receptionist print, stuff, address and mail the invites. Now he could relax and enjoy the party. Not that he really liked these party things.

He checked the attendance sheet at the reception table and saw that there were quite a few women's names without a matching name partner. Aha, maybe there were some single ladies coming who might be fun. Someone named Ann was listed with a question mark. What the heck did that mean? He signed in, picked up his name tag, and went to find a table. He saw some of his surgeon buddies, and they chatted for a while. He kept scanning the room, looking for women coming in alone, but each time he spied one, they'd be met by a man who'd probably let her off at the door and went to park the car.

It wasn't like he really needed to make a connection tonight, but his last girlfriend hadn't worked out, and he was looking for a replacement. He had really fallen for her, but Shari was a high powered businesswoman, had first taken a job in another city, and then moved to Spain. So he figured if a single woman came to this posh affair with a large donation required for admission, she wouldn't be impressed by men of celebrity and means. Hence, a better candidate for romance. Well, that was his plan, anyway.

He happened to be carrying his drink past the reception table when a breathless woman, fashionably late, arrived when the cocktail hour was almost over. He overheard her inquiring if she could still turn in her check and come in. Straining to hear, he was pleased to note the volunteer told her no problem, wrote out a nametag, and the woman turned slightly as she peeled off the backing and placed it on the bodice of her sequined cocktail dress. Ann. Hey, that was the question mark lady! And she was beautiful! That gave him an idea.

3

"Ann, I'm so glad you could make it! I've been watching for you!" Kevin said.

She looked confused. "Um, you are....?"

"Kevin! And you're Ann, right? I have a seat saved for you at the perfect table."

He led her, slightly dazed, to a table near the front, and she stopped several times to hug various women they passed by. Hmmm, did she know everybody?! He waited patiently, led her to the seat by his, pulled out the chair for her, and she seated herself.

Before she could arrange her thoughts to ask how he knew her, he started in with questions about her and her interest in this fundraiser and learned that her husband had died recently. Oh, that explained her wedding ring. He had noticed it and was wondering if he'd made a mistake. Hmmm, that meant she was vulnerable. Dead husband, still grieving, all alone, wealthy enough to attend this event. Good enough, Kevin concluded.

He went on full speed ahead, charming her with tales of his renown, funny anecdotes of amusing patients, all the stories people liked to hear, putting him in a positive light. She seemed to get sucked in the more he talked, and he noticed she was barely eating her dinner. They chatted, she shared, he listened, he asked a lot of questions, and it looked like Ann was quite interested.

Man, she was beautiful. Lovely dark brown hair, shoulder length. Brown eyes, but he noticed when he leaned in to listen to her, they sparkled with little flecks of green. Barely any makeup, but just enough that she looked like a model. And her smile, wow....he could feel himself drowning in her smile. This just might turn out to be a great evening.

Dinner was cleared away by staff, people visited the silent auction tables, and Kevin browsed the items alongside Ann. She pointed out the throw-sized quilt she had donated, and he was impressed. It had been bid up to $100 so far, but Ann confided she hoped it would go for much more. He

4

stepped up, scribbled his name and bid $150. That should impress her, he thought. As they traveled down the tables, admiring the jewelry, gift certificates, pottery and artwork, he glanced over his shoulder and noticed some woman adding a bid below Kevin's name on the quilt. Whew, he thought.

Then the emcee tapped on the microphone and tried to get everyone's attention. There was still time for bidding, but the speeches were about to begin. Kevin steered Ann back to their table, and the hospital auxiliary muckety-mucks started to spout their statistics. As the speeches droned on, he tried not to yawn, but noted Ann's eyes were bright, and she was very attentive. He started checking his Rolex every ten minutes or so, and finally decided the time was right.

"Listen, Ann, I have to run. I still have a patient to check in on tonight."

"So late?" Her eyes widened.

"Unfortunately, yes" he said. "Can you meet me at Starbucks at 10? The one on Monroe Street?"

"They're open that late?"

"Oh yes, they're there til after midnight. Can you be there? These speeches will be over by 9:30 or so."

Ann faltered. "Um, I….well, maybe…."

"Oh, come on, we'll have a few laughs, drink fancy coffee, it'll be fun!" He saw the start of a smile. And he added "I'm buying!"

She grinned. "Well, I want to stay until after the auctions close. But sure, why not? 10 pm at Starbucks on Monroe Street!"

"Great," Kevin said. "See you later!" He took her hand, kissed it gently on the back, European-style, and walked away. He turned back to look at her, and she seemed dazzled.

His patient didn't require much time, so he ended up at the coffee shop at 9:45, since it was so near downtown. He sat down facing the door, checked his phone for messages, and got busy answering texts and emails. When he looked up again, it was 10:15. Fashionably late again, he thought. That's okay, this gal seemed worth waiting for. But when she still hadn't arrived by 10:45, he had lost his patience. Kevin wasn't used to being blown off, and this was completely unacceptable. He grabbed his phone and stormed out. So much for this Ann character. Her loss.

You there, Elaine?

Yup. What's up?

Weird thing happened. I went to charity thing last night, met a handsome, wonderful man. A doctor!

Yay! Is there a But?

There sure is! We really connected at dinner. I could hardly eat it, it was so fattening, but he was so interesting. And he asked me out!

Where's the But?

We were supposed to meet at Starbucks on Monroe Street. I waited for a half hour, and he never showed!

The Starbucks Downtown?

No, the Starbucks Uptown. Wait. There are 2 Starbucks on Monroe Street?!?!?!?!?

Sure are! He was probably at the other one, near the hospital.

Oh crap.

Just call him! It's an easy mistake!

7

I don't have his number. Or
even his last name! Oh, this
is not good.

Don't worry about it! Plenty of fish
in the sea. I'm just really glad you're open
to meeting men. It'll be good for you.

Yeah, right. I'm not even
sure why I had accepted his
invitation....

Ann woke up feeling out of sorts today. The mix up with that doctor guy was just weird. She wasn't even sure if she should be dating yet. Pete's death was such a shock, and all the red tape of hospital and funeral bills, making decisions on cemetery plots and headstone, notifying everyone, had exhausted her. She was finally thinking it was time to enter the real world again, because she felt lonely.

She studied herself in the bathroom mirror. She still didn't see any gray in her brown hair, but she was vigilant. Her mother had gone gray young, so Ann figured she would too. Her face was still smooth and youthful looking. Now that she had started losing weight and increased the number of dancing and exercise classes, she could see definition in her leg muscles, and her stomach paunch was shrinking. Pete had been proud of her commitment to staying on the path to weight reduction. He knew how she hated how she looked, and she told him over and over she was jealous how he still weighed the same as he did in college.

As she brushed her teeth, she recollected how he had read that anecdote in the paper about a husband who had passed away, and how before he died, he had always squeezed the toothpaste on his wife's toothbrush when he got up before her. Ever since that day, Pete had done that for her. When he was out of town for a few days, she would think of him fondly when she had to squeeze her own toothpaste....it wasn't that it was so much work, but sheesh, how sweet is that when a man does that for his woman?! And now nobody did that for her. She sighed.

She and Pete had never discussed death or dying. She had no idea how he would feel about her looking for male friends now that he was gone. Neither of them had ever considered the possibility that one of them would die before they turned fifty. When they were dating seriously in college, they had talked about their future together, and had hashed out all the details. Where they'd live, what kind of house they'd buy, how long they'd wait before having children. Even who would do the cooking, cleaning, grocery shopping, and who'd pay the bills. They had followed their life plans right up until Pete had died.

They traveled. Sometimes she would accompany him on his trips to seminars. Many states far from home. Plus to France, England, Amsterdam and Italy. And to Germany, many times. But she didn't really love the traveling. Worrying about schedules. Plane security. Long waits. What had she forgotten? How fattening would the food be….would she gain weight? And then in the city of the seminar, Pete would leave her for the conference, and at first, she would go out sightseeing by herself. Several times, she had ventured out alone. Although she had enjoyed seeing the sights, trying to get back to the hotel was stressful. In one city, she couldn't find her note with the hotel address, and trying to communicate in another language she didn't know, was impossible. The cab driver drove her around for an hour until she recognized the building. So on later trips, she would just hole up in their hotel room while Pete was gone.

Finally, she stopped traveling with him, and was almost glad now that she had, as she had gotten used to living alone now and then, which ironically, was good practice. The adjustment of Pete's absence now was less traumatic than it could have been if she had never been in the house by herself.

Her friends couldn't fathom how neither Pete nor Ann had to work. They couldn't grasp the concept of being wealthy enough to live their lives the way they wanted. She had told and retold her friends the story of Pete developing something valuable while in college; it was a new audio compression algorithm that allowed music files to be small and easily transferred. She smiled to herself when she remembered how Pete had tried to explain it all to her, but she required many explanations until it sunk in. His technology was the precursor to the, now common, MP3 file. And he was still in high demand at seminars for his expertise. She finally gave up on explaining to her friends. "It's hard to understand," she'd say. "He was in the right place at the right time, and he was able to sell his invention for lots of money." Ann was always vague about how much, but if they knew how many zeroes there were in the payment, she was afraid they would line up for handouts.

She threw off her nightgown and stepped into the shower. Ann had seen some TV show once that talked about how someone had died from drowning while showering. Something about them having a seizure, collapsing, and their body blocking the drain. So they had drowned in the water that accumulated….apparently it only took a few inches if you're face down. She remembered telling the story to Pete, and she was afraid he would make fun of her for being fearful that it could happen to her. Or him. And neither of them was at risk for seizures! But instead of teasing her, he solemnly vowed he would stay nearby while she showered so he could make sure she was alright. She still thought of this when showering alone.

That was the kind of guy he was, Ann thought as she finished up, turned off the water and started toweling herself off. He would kill spiders for her (a wolf spider had landed on her as a teenager, and that fear still stayed with her), and protect her from the neighbor's kids when their tricycles careened past them on the sidewalk while they were walking. Pretty much, Pete was her protector, lover, soulmate and best friend.

She picked up her nightgown and hung it on the bathroom door hook. She studied her clothes in the closet. Ann had always been a careful dresser, coordinating colors and accessories, only considering clothing that was well made. As a sewer, she knew how to sew clothing, and was quite proficient at tailoring, hemming, and even making garments. But when she had discovered quilting, her interest in sewing clothes had waned. And now that she attended Fat Busters meetings, her excess weight was melting away, and her beautiful clothes just hung on her.

She had been shopping "on the secondary market" as her size began dropping, and haunted rummage and garage sales, consignment shops and estate sales. The thought of altering her existing wardrobe didn't interest her, though, as it would take time away from her quilting and other activities. Now that her clothing size had stabilized, she had been clothes shopping in stores, and was having a blast choosing her new wardrobe. Pete would have been so proud of her for dropping from a 2X to a size 8.

Ann continued to stare at her clothes as she slipped on her new bra and underwear. Even that category of items had gotten too big on her! What did it really matter what she wore? Who would see it? Why bother? She sighed. She used to dress to please Pete. He was so appreciative of her appearance, and it gave her great joy to try on a new outfit for him, twirling in front of him for his low whistle and smile.

So now what? Ann considered this. If her husband had been so wonderful, and everything she had ever wanted or needed, why did she even entertain the notion that she should still dress nicely to attract another man? Could another man ever fill the hole in her life?

She selected a slimming pair of black pants with tapered legs. That style always seemed to minimize her weight. A silver tunic she had purchased recently seemed to compliment the pants, so she carefully removed the tag with her manicure scissors and slipped it on over her head, down over her bra and smoothed it carefully into place.

"Let's face it," Ann said to her reflection, "You still care how you look. For Pete, or for anyone. You're not gonna change!"

Triumphant, she quickly made her bed, and tried not to look at Pete's side. She walked down the hall to where the digital scale sat in the guest room. Gleaming black, it so threatened her, and was the bane of her existence since she had started this weight loss thing. She hesitantly stepped on. Hmmm. It wasn't going down fast enough for her liking, but she had vowed to stick this out until she reached her goal weight. She stole another look in a mirror, the full length one on the back of the guest room door. She wasn't fat. Her friends thought she had lost enough already. But she still had about another five pounds to go.

It seemed so silly to weigh herself with clothes on, but she certainly couldn't strip for her Fat Busters meetings, so she usually selected lightweight clothing on weigh-in day. But that wasn't today, so she made a mental note that this new tunic was too heavy to wear for weigh-ins.

Ann stole a peek in her quilting studio as she passed by. So much fabric, batting, rulers, notions, thread. Quilts everywhere in various stages of progress. So much money invested. But when Pete's widowed mom had passed away, all the family fortune had gone to him, and their nest egg grew even more. Shrewd investing ensured that they could both live quite comfortably for the rest of their lives.

Except that Pete didn't have much life left. He had bought a hefty life insurance policy when they first got engaged, and the payoff was a staggeringly high amount. She could continue to live her life the way she wanted, doing volunteer work, going to guild meetings, and embracing the hobbies she adored. Was it too soon to get back in the swing of things? Should she really consider getting out there and meeting men?!

As she went down the stairs to the kitchen, she chastised herself for being sad. Life was still good. She had enjoyed a wonderful marriage with Pete. They had led fun, engaging lives. Their son, Connor, was a joy.

Pete had puttered in his workshop, creating gorgeous wood furniture. Their home, er, her home, she corrected herself, was full of things he had made: tables, headboards, chests of drawers, quilt racks, and more. He amused himself for hours doing genealogy research on both their families, and he loved watching old movies at home. 'Black and white, men in hats,' she had teasingly called them. Sometimes she would sit next to him on the plush gray sofa they had picked out together, and they would hold hands while watching. Some of the old stuff wasn't even half bad.

He managed their money on his laptop, and she felt grateful now that he made sure she understood all the sites, knew the passwords, and had a list of all the financial advisors, their phone numbers and their email addresses. That had come in very handy dealing with the red tape of Pete's death, transferring accounts to her name alone, and knowing what could be liquidated for daily expenses. Ann could really commiserate with widows in dealing with money issues after their spouses' deaths. Luckily for her, worrying about finances was not a problem she shared with many other women.

In the kitchen, she mixed up her nonfat Greek yogurt and blueberries for breakfast, and looked at herself one more time, this time in the reflective surface of the toaster.

"Well, Ann, if you're so lonely, if you miss Pete so much, then maybe you should get out there and find a friend to spend time with!" Her reflection grimaced back at her, and she glanced at the calendar as she brought her bowl to the table. Ukulele jam session tonight. Line dancing tomorrow night. Yikes. She grabbed her cell and texted her friend and neighbor, Debby.

So I'm considering going to my jam session tonight. Haven't practiced much, but they say music soothes the savage beast.

Or something like that. You should go. Put down the phone and go practice. Don't embarrass yourself.

I'd really like to see that guy who sits next to me---he's so encouraging. Maybe I'll have better luck with HIM than the sorta no-show doctor. I'll have to tell you about that.

Just go, Ann. Call me when you can.

Rod sauntered through the library, swinging his bag. He considered picking out a few novels for his business trip that night but knew he didn't have enough time. He glanced at the wall clock as he passed the checkout desk and frowned. Crap, he was late.

It'd be easier if he still wore a watch, but his buddies had laughed at him, calling him a dinosaur. "Why wear a watch, Rod? You've got a phone!" they'd taunt. "Sell that puppy on Craig's List, my friend, or you'll be the last human being on the planet to wear a watch!" Every time he looked at his wrist, they made fun of him.

So he had succumbed, and found himself running late wherever he went. He'd sneak a look at his cell phone during a meeting, at the car dash while driving, or when he passed the bank's electronic clock. But pulling out his phone was too damned time consuming just to see the time.

Naturally, he grumbled to himself. Now he was late to the jam session. He was hoping to see that cute chick he'd noticed the last few sessions. She had been sitting alone in the second row the night he first saw her, so he had slipped into the seat next to her. She struggled to set up her music stand, he remembered, and he had helped her. They had chatted, and she was so pretty. He sat next to her from then on, and she was very easy to talk to.

But now everyone was seated, and everyone was done tuning their ukes, and announcements had begun. There were hardly any seats left, so he sat in the last row behind where he normally sat. He hardly listened as the leader droned on about the upcoming schedule, the Facebook page, and their lending library. God, that lady in charge was so boring. He preferred lively women, like the one with the finicky music stand. She had kept apologizing for making him work, and her smile just lit up her face. Maybe he should ask her out, he was thinking at the time.

Now, just as they were starting their first song, he felt his phone vibrate, and pulled it out of his pocket. Crap! His flight was moved up an hour. He had to hightail it out of there to get to the airport on time. This is unbelievable! Can the airline do this?!? As the strains of The Lion Sleeps Tonight

16

strummed through the room, he grabbed his music bag, stuffed his uke back in, and dashed for the meeting room exit.

Looking at his empty wrist yet again, he still knew he had no time to make any apologies for his hasty exit. He rushed through the library lobby for the door to the parking lot, grumbling to himself about the schedule change.

Aw, hell, Rod thought as he jumped into his car and gunned it outta there, screw everything. This job with all the traveling sucks. He'll look for a different job when he gets back in town. And maybe he'd been looking for love in all the wrong places. He might as well forget the stupid ukulele…he always liked guitars better anyway.

Ann had always been a chatty girl, wanting to be the center of attention. Her parents felt it was partly because she had no siblings and was doted on a great deal. But it was obvious early on that this girl had enormous theatrical tendencies. She had a clear, strong voice. School officials tapped her even in elementary school to narrate orchestra concerts and plays. For a young girl to speak with such authority was unusual, and her parents assumed acting was in their daughter's future. So they encouraged Ann to try out for all the community and scholastic performances, and Ann was always chosen to be front and center. She wasn't shy or nervous in front of people and was calm and assured speaking in front of ten people or an audience of 500.

Crafts were a big thing in Ann's upbringing, too, as her mom did flower arranging, sewed garments, quilts and home decorating items, and could knit and crochet. It was inevitable that Ann would learn these skills too, and learn she did. Sewing costumes and dress-up clothing was fun for her. The pageantry of her plays and performances was more fun when she could share in the creation of the regalia. Her mom had a fondness for hats, and Ann shared the joy of creating a persona with different headgear.

In fourth grade, Ann and her mom discovered a magazine pattern for Noah and his ark, with pairs of little felt animals. They enthusiastically sewed up their prototypes, and the little animals were so adorable. When Ann proudly brought them into school to show her friends, girls would squeal with delight and want to buy little sets of animals of their own. So Ann began taking orders, and a little cottage industry was run each evening in their craft room, the two of them cutting out the shapes, sewing them together, stuffing with bits of fiber, hand-sewing them closed, and embroidering little eyes, noses and details. At the price of fifty cents to one dollar each, they hardly produced a huge profit, but it was fun, and a project 'the girls' could do together. Ann learned valuable lessons in entrepreneurship, creativity and deadlines.

As well, Ann embraced dancing, gymnastics and all sorts of exercising. Ann's grades weren't stellar, but they were acceptable. She was able to get by in her classes and still have time for all her activities. Ann's mother didn't work outside the home while her daughter was young, so she was free to shuttle Ann around to all her goings-on. Brownies, then Girl Scouts. Play practice. Sewing and piano lessons. Ballet and music theory. Eventually, Ann began getting choosier with her time, and she dropped ballet and piano, but took up ukulele. She sewed many of her own clothes and made pillows and quilts to give as gifts.

Ann's dad was an optometrist, and his office was next to their home, attached by a breezeway. Part of their front lawn was blacktopped as a parking lot, and patients would come and go, never disturbing the occupants of the private residence. Ann was never as close to her dad as she was with her mom, but father and daughter still had a special bond. Ann had been learning in school about the serious effects of cigarettes and nagging her dad about quitting wasn't doing any good. They made a deal when Ann was 13: she would stop biting her nails if he would stop smoking. Amazingly, it worked; both bad habits were dropped. Ann always felt for years afterward that she got the better deal....getting her father to live a longer healthier life.

Neither dogs nor cats were on Ann's radar. Her mother was allergic to animal fur, so they had always owned a parakeet. Actually, birds were the perfect pet for a little chatterbox like Ann. She would spend hours with Chirpy on her finger, solemnly repeating words and phrases. The bird would nestle his little head under her nose, his beak pressed against the hollow over Ann's lip, and listen carefully. "Pretty birdy," "I love you," and "gimme a kiss." Later in his cage, he would practice the phrases until he got them right. People hearing Chirpy talking always commented how much he sounded like Ann.

When Chirpy died, they bought another Chirpy and Ann would work with the new bird on talking. Chirpy the third joined the family when Ann was a teenager, and this parakeet was the best talker of them all. He learned to say, "birds don't talk, birds chirp!" and "beam me up, Scotty." It was fun coming up with creative phrases to teach him; family and friends would contribute ideas for what to teach the bird. "There's no place like home," "onward and upward," and "what's for dinner?" were quickly mastered by the little parakeet.

Dating wasn't a big part of Ann's life. She had lots of girlfriends, and lots of boy friends, that is, friends who were boys. But her social group tended to go out together as a group, to plays, to the mall, out for dinner. Ann always had dates to the special dances like homecoming. She wasn't impressed by the 'jocks', but rather, tended to like the brainy guys, the ones in the computer club, school newspaper, chess team, and audio-visual club. She may not have understood all they knew, but she could identify with those students more.

They lived in a suburb outside of Buffalo, New York. It was the best of both worlds, being able to enjoy a small town where people knew each other, and enjoyed community picnics, fairs and festivals. But it was a short drive to downtown Buffalo to see professional theatrical productions, concerts or sporting events. Ann's parents felt it was a great place to raise a family. But no siblings came along to round out the family after Ann. No mention was ever made of the subject, but Ann's mom would often say she wished her daughter were twins. It wasn't until much later in life, Ann would realize what that meant. She vowed to be the best only child to her parents that she could be.

So she was hesitant when it came time to choose a university. Growing up, it was always said 'when you go to college'; never 'if you go to college'. Her dad had done his undergraduate work at State U in Ohio, before he went on to get his optometric degree. He felt his alma mater was a fine choice for his daughter. Ann wasn't too keen about being a five-hour drive away from her folks, but they encouraged her to spread her wings. Truth be told, she wasn't even too thrilled with the idea of further education. She had no idea what she wanted to be when she grew up. And she wasn't even sure what university would accept her with her mediocre grades. Her parents and school counselor assured her that all her extracurricular activities would count in her favor, so Ann applied to State U early admission, which promised she would apply nowhere else, and would attend if accepted. It worked, and Ann received the fat acceptance envelope early in her senior year of high school. She would be moving to Ohio.

"Onward and upward," Chirpy said.

Blog: Therefore I Quilt

Why We Love to Sew!

Posted: Feb 14, 2017 11:43 AM EST

Surrounding ourselves with quilting magazines, gadgets and patterns is fun! Nothing compares with the thrill of wandering around a store by the bolts of fabric, running our hands over the soft cottons, admiring the array of colors, petting the plush flannels. There's something magical about turning a pile of fabric and thread into a completed quilt. We like the crackle of paper patterns, the challenge of complicated directions that we actually understand and the comfort of the occasional easy-to-follow directions for small projects. We get a thrill from discovering a new template or notion that makes things easier, too. We have learned to master our sewing machines, and their efficient whir empowers us. We appreciate the compliments we get from others, we like saving money by creating our own items, and we feel empowered by our abilities. Our homemade quilts warm our family and friends. And of course, the camaraderie of our sewing friends is like the icing on the cake, and we're all proud to be each other's support group. Because each of us truly understand how we all feel about this wonderful hobby of sewing!

~Ann

The American Legion hall parking lot was full, as usual, and Joe parked his pickup in one of the last spots of the third row. He tried to appear confident as he entered the building and followed the music to the party room where the dancers were assembling. He scanned the room, looking for Ann, but he was nervous about his decision to finally ask her out. They had been getting to know one another during the breaks, and he knew she was single, available, and he thought, pretty hot.

Joe had considered not coming tonight; he'd been feeling crummy all day, and figured he was coming down with something. Shake it off, man, he thought…this girl could be the answer to your prayers!

He had been lonely since moving to town, and there weren't many like-minded souls like him at work, in his apartment complex, or anywhere he shopped or went. Until he discovered this line dancing class he saw advertised on the local grocery store bulletin board. He had taken a chance and showed up. To his surprise, there were other guys in cowboy hats, dusty boots, blue jeans and western shirts, just like him, at these dances, and he felt like he had come home. He was getting to know the other dancers, both men and women, and everyone was so friendly.

And now, if he also scored a girlfriend there, life would be pretty good! Each time he had thought about getting up the nerve to ask her out, he was pretty sure he couldn't go through with it. He'd always been kinda shy, and he kept thinking, what if she turned him down? He wasn't sure he could handle that.

But Joe was resolved to make tonight the night. He'd even planned what to say, and how to say it. Cripes, he felt like he was back in junior high. Man up, guy, he told himself, just act natural. He kept dancing to each song, knowing the steps, confident at least in that. He'd learned so many dances back home in Nashville, and hooking his thumbs through his Levis' belt loops, he tried to remain calm, watching the door and waiting, concentrating on his footwork. Cross rock, turn and shuffle. K step. Out out in in.

He kept craning his neck, watching the door for Ann. Leanna came in, the one who sings along to every song. She was with Rochelle, that advanced dancer who seemed like she was slumming being at these dances. And there was Ranjana; he had helped her with her steps a few times. No Ann.

The leader called out the dances, running through the steps. Mambo. Coaster step. Jazz box. Vine and hitch. His confidence grew. But his stomach was churning, and he didn't think it was nerves. Dang, maybe he really was getting sick. Why tonight, of all nights?

Joe couldn't concentrate on the lessons. He recalled the first time he and Ann had connected during line dancing. She had stumbled a bit on a kick ball chain and ended up kinda kicking his ankle. She had been so embarrassed and wouldn't stop apologizing. He was more concerned with whether she was okay from her stumble, and they laughed about her clumsiness during the break. He was dazzled by her smile and did everything he could to keep her smiling.

He started watching her the following Thursday nights, and did his best at finding things to talk about with her. When she went down the hall to the canteen (why was the American Legion bar called a canteen? he wondered) he would follow and help her carry her armload of water bottles back to the party room. The policy there was, no outside drinks allowed. Probably to get more revenue for the Legion, he supposed. Ann's friends didn't like spending so much for bottles of water, so Ann occasionally stepped up to buy rounds of water for the ladies at her table. That was so nice of her, Joe thought. She was just so NICE. The sort of woman who'd be perfect for him. Not aggressive. Polite. Pretty. Well dressed, with no trashy low-cut stuff. A classy gal, all around.

His mind snapped back to the lessons and the dancing. Rock, recover. Heel jacks. Scissor step. Rocking chair. Man, the guys from work would make fun of him for his love of dancing. He didn't care…. dancing gave him confidence he didn't normally have. If he could find a like-minded female, he could even strut his stuff at two stepping. Joe nodded at Richard, the cool dude who rocked a t shirt and baggy jeans. That guy looked so self-assured, like he didn't have a care in the world. Rumba box. Cross rock. Hook.

He felt his gut lurch again and was getting concerned. Think healthy, he told himself. Don't get sick tonight. Just hold on. But a bead of sweat began dripping down his forehead from behind his cowboy hat. Man up, Joe thought.

Another bunch of people came in, paid their admission and joined the dancing. Joy, who did the minimal amount of movement possible. Mary, the lady who smiled the whole time. Tony, who kept his thumbs permanently hooked in his belt loops…maybe they kept his pants from falling down! And there was John and Viv, a really nice couple he had talked to a few times. Wait, over by the wall, was that Ann? Joe craned his neck as he did the twinkle steps (who named that step, anyway?!?), but no, it was Rae Jean, the lady who always ended up facing the wrong wall while dancing. She was a friend of Ann's; he could ask her later, if Ann never showed.

Now Joe felt a definite rumbling in his bowels, and he suspected the worst. Just hold on, man, he chided himself, you can do this. Tonight's the night. You're gonna turn your lonely life around, I tell ya!

So much for his resolve, he thought, when he finally saw Ann come in. She was alone, as she always was. He couldn't have handled it if she were part of a whole gang of women, laughing and clutching their friends' arms like the others did. He was halfway through dancing the Wagon Wheel with the crowd, and he faltered, watching her count out her singles into the till by the door for the evening's dance. She strode confidently across the room, depositing her purse on a table and joining the dancers to finish out the number.

Ann danced like an angel. So graceful. So beautiful. She smiled at him when she saw him, and that pushed him over the edge….yes, he was gonna ask her out. He wanted to maneuver over to where she danced, but didn't want to appear too obvious, so he tried to play it cool. He felt the sweat

25

continue to trickle out from under the band of his hat, and worried it wasn't from the dancing, or from seeing Ann. He felt his stomach twisting and started to fret again that he had picked up some bug.

No, not tonight, he told himself firmly. Let me just get through this social situation, and he promised himself, he could get sick tomorrow, but just not tonight. Damn, why was he such a shy jerk? Joe tried to boost his confidence, but it was careening in the other direction. Let me get through this dance, let me make it through the break, please God, let me get through talking to Ann, just hang in there, he kept telling himself.

All though Boot Scootin' Boogie, he felt the rumbling, the sweating, the weakness. Dancing Gypsy Queen, it got worse. It was painful cramping by the time they got to Honky Tonk Stomp. He knew he had to get to the bathroom, pronto. It was located all the way across the hall, and as he broke away from the other dancers, he trod purposefully, trying to appear casual. Luckily, the dancers were facing the other wall as he yanked open the men's room door and dashed for the stall. Maybe nobody had seen his urgency. Maybe he was okay.

But he fumbled with his belt, and before he could sit, the worst happened. Some of it went in the toilet, but way too much did not. Joe was in there a long time, struggling with the thin toilet paper, wiping and flushing. He threw open the stall door and started grabbing the flimsy paper towels, cleaning off the damage, rubbing at his jeans. He threw off his hat before it went into the mess.

This was bad. Very bad. He started smashing wet towels into the denim, hoping to make the mess disappear, but it only seemed to make it worse. He finally yanked off his boots, disgusted to see there even was a mess down the tooled leather. He peeled off the splotchy Levis, started rinsing out what he could in the sink, dragging towel shards over his boots, almost in tears at the terrible turn of events. But this wasn't working. If only he could teleport himself away from this embarrassment, this place, this crummy, stinky bathroom. Anywhere but here. There wasn't even a way to dry the jeans off.

Joe felt like he had been at this for an hour. Luckily, no other guy had come in. When he finally made himself as presentable as possible, he surveyed himself in the mirror and realized this was not meant to be. No way could he face people the way he smelled, the telltale water stains on his jeans. No way could he face Ann. This was turning out to be the most uncomfortable night of his life.

He grabbed his hat and peeked out the bathroom door, and through his watery eyes, he saw everybody dancing Little White Church. Yeah, pretty ironic, he grimly thought to himself, there'll never be a little white church in HIS future. When the dancers were facing the opposite direction, he sidled out the door, walked fast hugging the back wall, trying to slip out unnoticed. But he saw Rae Jean on the dance floor, facing the wrong way, and she looked right at him with a quizzical look. Well, sure, he was heading out instead of in. A bunch of women were coming back from the bar with their beers, heading right for him, and passed right by him to enter the hall. He kept his head down, trying to appear invisible, but he thought he saw one gal wrinkle her nose as she passed by. He almost ran out the exit to the parking lot.

As he grabbed an old towel out of the pickup's bed and arranged it on the driver's seat to protect it from his foul self, the tears started flowing. No way could he EVER go back to this place. He'd never set foot in this American Legion again. They saw him. They smelled him. Maybe one of those women who passed him were friends with Ann. He couldn't imagine ever facing any of these people one more time.

He peeled his damp truck keychain out of his pants pocket and jammed the key into the ignition. The truck roared to life, and he peeled out from his parking spot towards the exit. As he tore out of there for home, Joe resolutely swore to himself, he'd never line dance in this town ever. Maybe he should quit his job and move back to Nashville. Life sucks.

To: Betty <MommyOfAnn>
From: Ann <QuiltingFanatic>
Date: today

Hi, Mom. Sorry it's been so long since I've communicated. I hope your neighbor has recovered from her surgery by now and is back to exercise classes with you.

I'm still quilting like crazy. I find it very soothing to cut up fabric and sew it back together into something warm and cozy. It takes my mind off myself. I've also been sewing some clothing for an upcoming storytelling gig, I'll tell you more about it in a minute.

Connor is very happy in California. I admit I was extremely worried about him moving out there so young. But I can hardly criticize that, considering how young I was when I got married and moved! I've always regretted Pete and I didn't marry again in front of friends and family, like we promised. I hope you aren't upset we never got around to it….

Thanks for asking about my weight loss. Yes, I'm doing great with it, even with all the stress since Pete's death. I'm down over 50 pounds, and I've had a lot of fun picking out a new wardrobe! I still attend Fat Busters meetings regularly, so I know I'll get to my final goal soon. No, I'm not making my new clothes….I'd rather quilt!

Yeah, I'm back to all my old activities. And yes, I'm thinking about dating again, or at least, meeting a man to be friends with. I'll keep ya informed. So far, tho, any guy I've considered has sorta disappeared once I finally decided to approach him. Dating after all these years isn't easy, I can tell you! I think they call it ghosting? We talk, we really hit it off, and then they just drop out of sight. I'm considering using a dating website….what do you think? I've heard so many success stories from other people, that maybe it might work for me.

I've been talking on the phone a lot to this man I'm doing a historic reenactment with next weekend. He has done an amazing bunch of research and has our characters prepared. And I sewed up a historically accurate outfit to wear….I'll have to attach a photo after the weekend! Remember I told you about that whole resurrectionist project, and you called them grave robbers? They really existed, and it's pretty shocking that was so common in the old days. How sad that people would later go to visit their loved one's graves, not knowing that their loved one wasn't even in there!

And the best part is, this history guy is really nice, and I'm thinking about how we get along so well, over the phone, anyway. Makes me wonder if he might be for me. Aaaannd here I go, circling back to the topic of possibly going out with men.

So on that note, I think I'm finally ready to stop wearing my wedding ring. I've debated back and forth, but ultimately decided that if I'm going to consider entering the dating pool, I shouldn't appear as a married woman. Or a grieving widow. It's hard. Does this make me shallow? Or not respecting Pete's memory? We never had talked about it, but I kinda think Pete would have wanted me to marry again someday if anything happened to him. He sure didn't expect this scenario would come up so soon in our lives!

Anyway, I'll talk to you later….give my best to dad.

Bradley had belonged to his historical reenactment groups for a few years now when he decided to participate in the big encampment weekend everyone was always talking about. It sounded like an enriching experience, and a wonderful opportunity to share living history with the public.

He had been crazy about history in high school, got his best grades in those classes, and felt lucky he had great teachers who really made history come alive for their students. So, he majored in American History at college, and took part in all the related events he could, soaking up all the culture of days gone by. He began collecting historical costumes for the history days and enjoyed taking on the persona of another man in another time. He especially loved the challenge of memorizing a fixed body of facts and interpreting them into a character who could influence others. It was no surprise when he decided to become a high school history teacher. He had pledged to himself, he would always share that love of the human side of our nation's past with his students. Make it come alive for them like it did for him.

As a single guy, he kept himself busy evenings and weekends with his history guilds, working on committees in his free time. His local historical society friends were encouraging him to advocate for larger and more intricate projects. He started taking on board positions, moving up the ranks into the district and then state boards.

He had participated in cemetery tours and mini encampments. He had even performed for museum educators and professionals, enjoying enhancing other people's understanding.

But Bradley had never taken off work to immerse himself in a four-day encampment, living, sleeping, and eating as our forefathers used to live. Once he decided to take this giant leap, his reenactor friends were very reassuring, promising an enlightening and action-packed experience.

Bradley thought of himself as more of a living historian and was committed to getting every detail right. His friends sneered at those who didn't act this way, calling them farbs, or those 'far be it from authentic' actors who didn't care about accuracy. He promised himself he would create a historic persona who would impress his fellow actors and the audience as well. And he knew what role he wanted to play.

Resurrectionists thrived in our country's history, stealing bodies from freshly interred coffins and selling the corpses to physicians at medical schools. The only dissections allowed in those times were of dead bodies belonging to prisoners who died or who were condemned to death. Medical students desperately needed bodies to examine, to perfect their knowledge and surgery skills. Men who provided these specimens were paid well, and no questions were asked. They had their tools of the trade for opening the graves, pulling out the bodies with metal hooks and ropes. They were careful to leave undisturbed any jewelry or valuables left inside. Stealing such items would be a felony, whereas disturbing a grave was only a misdemeanor should they be caught.

Just as lucrative was removing the teeth of the corpses, selling them quietly to the local dentists to use in their patients' mouths to plug holes left by rotting or dead extracted teeth. And long braids of hair could be cut off and sold to craftsmen, who used the genuine hair to make wigs for those who needed them. The bounty of just one evening's work could net a fortune of more than what a common laborer could earn in six months.

Bradley had his outfit and the tools ready, but he needed a woman. He needed a woman to play his wife, actually. Most resurrectionists sent their wives out to scope out the burials, watching for any booby traps that might be inserted, for morticians knew of the danger of the body snatchers. The wife would hire herself out as a keener, or one who would attend the funeral. She'd be crying, wailing and keening as if she were truly distraught. It was a sign of wealth and respect to have many mourners, and the wives' incomes nicely supplemented their husbands' take for the work.

So he began the search for a woman who would play the part with him. He needed a good actress or storyteller, and if she could sew, so much the better, to make her costume. A roughhewn skirt, simple peasant shirt and apron would be suitable. He had the idea to find someone who lived in the city where the encampment took place; that would be ideal. She could go home to sleep, so he didn't have to provide her with a crude tent and sleeping quarters.

His state board contacts put him in touch with the storyteller association there, and several women were even recommended to him as being the most suitable for this role. As he lived three hours away, he conducted the interviews via email, phone and Skype, and decided on a pleasant woman named Ann. And best of all, she agreed to perform with him all four days of the encampment.

He taught her what her part would entail, and they began practicing on Skype several times each week. She held up her garments to the computer camera for him to see as she finished sewing each piece, and he was pleased with their appearance. He gave her advice on her hair, and made sure she agreed to wear no jewelry, makeup or nail polish. He feared the 'no makeup' rule would cause pushback, but Ann completely understood.

He showed her the "Professional Keener For Hire" sign, crudely drawn, that she would stand next to. He held up the large rusty hooks, the crowbar and ropes, but couldn't show her the spade, as it was still in his garage. He could tell she was getting quite excited at the impending performance, as was he.

As the day neared, their practices got a bit more frantic, and he prepared her for questions she might have to answer. About what keening was. How did they keep from getting caught. What kind of booby traps she looked for in the grave to tell her husband that night, before he went out to do his work. He coached her on playing up what a noble profession this was, providing a service to doctors learning about the workings of the human body. People today could thank resurrectionists for the abilities of their current-day surgeons.

Their last few Skype sessions were more relaxed, as she seemed completely ready. They began chatting about personal things. Her storytelling. His history students. Her quilting. She told him about her ukulele playing. He admitted to being a history nerd. They laughed easily together. And he felt really good about her playing his wife. Really great, actually. He very much admired her.

Dating had never been a priority for him, since he was so busy with his job during the day and history guilds evenings and weekends. But as the face time accumulated with this charming woman, he really began to care about her, and wondered if the feeling was mutual. They hadn't discussed any personal details; he didn't even know if she was married! She had never mentioned a husband, but they were always so focused on their rehearsals at first, it had never come up.

He had heard that at these long encampment things, it was so nice to relax, get out of the traffic and hustle bustle of daily living, and just live for the moment. The old, historical moment. Hmmm. Maybe what happens at encampment stays at encampment! The thought emboldened him. Ann was playing his wife….maybe he could sorta act like her husband?!? The thought thrilled him.

The big day arrived, and Bradley got to the site early. He unloaded his van, pitched his tent and checked the volunteer map for his resurrectionist scene location. Then he moved his van to the parking lot, walked back across the field and started preparing the 'graves' as visual aids at their scene, plumping them up with the topsoil he brought from home. He slipped the headstones in place, set up the keener sign and the small rough wooden table with the teeth and hair for showing the audience. He was ready. Except for his costume. And Ann.

It was still an hour before she was to arrive, so he went to his tent and unpacked his clothes. He slipped on his tunic and trousers, and remembered he still had to find a historically accurate pair of old shoes. He walked around to find a sutler who was already set up, knowing that an onsite merchant would have just the right footwear.

He discovered that quite a few were already open for business, and he searched through bins, looking for the oldest, rattiest pair of early Americana shoes. Yes, the perfect pair! And in his size! As he took them

33

to the checkout, he noticed trays of old, imitation 'authentic' jewelry, and his eyes lit on a simple gold ring. He knew that a simple man like a resurrectionist would probably sport a wedding band, so he threw in a few extra dollars to the merchant and slipped the band on his left ring finger.

Bradley returned to his station and started watching for her at the agreed upon time. He thought he saw her across the field, recognizing the crude plaid of the floor length skirt. As she approached, his face lit up. It was her! And she looked fantastic!

He ran up to her. "Ann! It's so nice to meet you! I'm Bradley!"

"Yes, I know. You look familiar!" Her smile lit up her soot-smudged face.

"Wow, the dirt is a nice touch," he said.

"Yeah," she said, "You never suggested it, but I figured your wife wouldn't be clean and tidy."

He backed up and they began walking over to the site. She admired his costume.

"What a handsome grave robber you are, Bradley!"

He smiled, and as they reached their spot, he turned to show her the setup. As he did, he caught a glimpse of her looking down at her left hand, frowning and slipping off her ring, sliding it into her apron pocket. A ring. A wedding ring. Damn. She WAS married. He had told her no jewelry, and she just remembered to take it off.

He felt sad. But he put a smile on his face as he turned back to her with the boxes of teeth and hair she would be showing to the audience. And for a split second, it looked like she focused on the gold band on his finger, before she reached out to take the boxes. No sense in mentioning to her it was just a prop.

Hey Elaine, you there?

Yeah, what's up?

One thing I forgot to tell you on the phone before: You know that storytelling gig I did over the weekend? My partner was a hunk, and I had really fallen for him, thinking I had a chance.

And?......

....and he turned out to be married. Maybe all the good ones are either married, or dead.

C'mon now, there are a lot of men out there who'd love to be with you. You're gorgeous! I'd be tempted if I weren't a woman. And straight.

LOL! You just want my quilting studio.

Yes, I do!   :-)

Well, I gotta finish packing for retreat. Sorry you have that cousins's wedding and can't attend, but I'll call you with all the hot gossip when we're both back.

"What happens at quilt retreat STAYS at quilt retreat"!

Ha!

35

BLOG: Therefore I Quilt

Why do you do it?

Posted: Apr 30, 2018 02:34 PM EDT

Ponder this intriguing question: Why do you quilt?

Perhaps it's the exciting possibilities when you see a pattern that motivates you. Or the tingle of creativity when you match up fabric with a plan and can't wait to get started. Or maybe your senses are inspired: the sight of rich reds and deep blues, plush in their promise, or the feel of soft flannels, waiting to be sewn together into a charity quilt. Possibly the sound of crisp cottons when you run your hands over them motivates you, or hearing the thrum of your sewing machine, performing efficiently.

You like the feeling of satisfaction when you have neat piles of cut pieces, ready for sewing together. The accomplishment when a block is done, then a row, then a top. Then the anticipation of the layering, quilting, finishing...each step is so rewarding. And finally, cuddling under that beautiful, warm quilt is so fulfilling! Perhaps the challenge is what drives you: mastering a tricky pattern, perfect quilting stitches, winning a show ribbon. Of course, the camaraderie of sharing time with other sewers is a big draw. Sew-ins, charity sews and quilt retreats beckon....in fact, my guild retreat is coming up! I can't wait!

In cold wintry weather, maybe you like that this sewing hobby is done indoors, cozy and toasty warm. Or you get such happiness giving away a quilt you made with your own two hands. Perhaps you quilt because the moment when the binding is completely finished and the quilt is done empowers you. You did it! You're a quilter!

Why do YOU quilt?

~Ann

Beth was nervous as she dragged her suitcases into the hotel. She had never been to a quilt retreat before, but she heard there were openings for non-members at the retreat sponsored by the quilt guild a couple of towns over from hers. They had announced this at her quilt guild a few months ago, and her ears had perked up. She had heard great things about that event: how they had skits, quilty rummage sales, door prizes galore, free tables, demos and more. She had checked their website, downloaded the registration form, filled it out and sent it in with her check. She had requested a roommate so the hotel room would be cheaper, and the chairman had assigned her one. Someone named Ann.

Then it was time, so Beth packed more fabric, kits, templates and rulers, thread, quilting notions and patterns than she had clothes. Her sewing machine was safely ensconced in her rolling tote, and she was pumped to attend her first retreat. Nobody else from her guild was attending, which was a shame, so she had to drive the two hours alone. No matter, Beth thought, this was time off work, and promised to be a fun, relaxing weekend.

After checking in, she read through her welcome packet, found her spot in the sewing room, and started unpacking her sewing gear. The ladies who were already there seemed so nice, and everyone welcomed her warmly, calling her a retreat newbie. Then she took her suitcase of clothes and toiletries up to her assigned hotel room and unpacked that stuff as well. Her roommate wasn't there yet, so she went back downstairs to sew.

Time flew by, as there were demos, drawings, and announcements, and she enjoyed laughing at the nearby conversations and cheerful joking. She was working on a Snail's Trail design in red, white and blue that she planned on donating to Quilts of Valor when (if?) she got the whole quilt done.

Just as dinner was announced, someone tapped her on her shoulder, and she whirled around to see a pleasant looking woman wearing a nametag that said Ann.

"You must be my roomie!" the woman said.

38

"Oh, yes, I've been waiting for you!" Beth said. Ann explained her normal roommate was out of town for a wedding, so was glad she was available to room with someone new this weekend. They walked to dinner together and started compared notes on their quilting experience and guild positions, but they were at the dining room so quickly, they hardly got started when they arrived. The two of them pulled up chairs at the same table, and everyone introduced themselves to the newbie Beth. The ladies at their table were a hoot; Beth thought she'd pee her pants, she was laughing so hard at their stories!

After dinner, everyone returned to the sewing room, and the free door prize tickets were distributed to each participant. Her tablemates saw her inquisitive look and explained she should put her name on the back of all the tickets, then put them into the little bags taped by the door prizes she wanted to win. This way Beth could decide if she wanted to throw them into lots of different bags, or just a few, to improve her odds of winning. She scribbled her name many times (hmmm, shoulda brought address labels, like the other women!), joined the throng swarming around the prizes, and was delighted at all the goodies she could possibly win. Rotary blade sharpener. Fat quarter packs. Flannel yardages. Quilting novels. Stacks of quilt magazines, tied together in bundles. Spools of expensive thread. A new quilt kit…yikes, that was such an expensive prize! The piles and bags went on and on, and it was overwhelming! She finally tore the tickets apart on the perforations and just randomly tossed them in bags, sure she wouldn't win anything.

By midnight, many of the ladies had said goodnight and retired up to their rooms. Beth tidied up her sewing area and counted the blocks she had finished: twenty-two…hooray! Then she checked her pattern, and realized she'd need a total of eighty. Wow, this sucker would take some time!

The room was dark when Beth let herself into the hotel room, and Ann appeared to be asleep. So, she tried to be very quiet as she got ready for bed and slipped into her beautifully made bed across the room. Such an indulgence, fresh soft sheets that someone else had made up! Beth was asleep almost instantly, she was so exhausted.

In the morning, Ann was already gone. Beth was a bit embarrassed that she had slept later than she planned. The hotel continental breakfast was available for another thirty minutes, so she hurriedly showered, dressed and hustled downstairs.

The day was a blur for Beth of meals, laughter and prize drawings. Sweet....she won a pack of fabric and two spools of lightweight bobbin thread! And now there was another set of prizes, bags and tickets set out for another round of possible wins....wow! And there were demos, skits, snacks, lots more laughter, oh, and loads of sewing! She couldn't believe how much fun she was having, and how friendly everybody was. The pattern repeated itself late that night, of Beth quietly letting herself into the hotel room after midnight, and Ann quietly slumbering in her bed across the room. Gee, roommates didn't even have to get along here if they never even saw each other!

And when Beth awoke Sunday morning, she was sad that the retreat would be finishing up that day. Again, Ann was already gone, so once more Beth got ready quickly to rejoin all her new friends for the final round of sewing and fun. At breakfast, the quilters were planning a nature walk later to get some much-needed exercise, and Beth promised her table mates she would join them. As she walked back to the sewing room, Ann passed her and grabbed her arm.

"Oh, Beth! I'm glad I saw you!" Ann's eyes sparkled. "We haven't had enough time together, and there's something I want to talk to you about!"

"Sure thing, Ann. Let's meet on the walk later. I want to talk to you, too!" Maybe she could finally get to know this mysterious roommate lady!

The next few hours passed quickly as Beth sewed more of her quilt blocks, watched a demo on fast bargello charity quilts and listened to the last door prize drawings. Nothing this time for her, darn! The happy chatter turned to soft murmuring, as many participants were leaving on their exercise hike, so she wrapped up her sewing, tidied up and looked around for who was still available. Ann appeared at her side. "Ready to walk? I have quite a proposition for you!"

Beth was a bit apprehensive at that but grabbed her cardigan sweater from the back of her sewing chair and followed Ann out the back door. The other ladies weren't in sight. The two quilters strolled towards the woods, chatting about what they had gotten done, and how sad it was the weekend retreat was almost over. Beth wanted to ask Ann if she could show her the one-step double fold binding technique other quilters had mentioned, but she couldn't get a word in edgewise as Ann chattered away about the guild.

As they left the clearing and entered the wooded area, the path narrowed, and the women had to walk closer together. Beth still couldn't see the others, and she began to feel uneasy walking shoulder to shoulder with this woman. What did she mean 'proposition'? A sudden jolt of awakening hit her, and she stopped and turned to face Ann, ready to insist she wasn't interested in her 'that way'.

Ann, too, halted abruptly, trained her sparkling eyes on Beth, and they both stared at each other silently. The silence went on a beat too long, and with their eyes locked on each other, the trees seemed to close in around them. Beth's lips parted hesitantly, about to explain, but she couldn't find her voice. At that, Ann leaned closer and her lips pursed slightly. Magnetized by those eyes, Beth brought her face even closer, swept away by whatever was happening.

Their lips were so close, their shared heat seemed electrifying. Both women seemed to feel that a kiss was inevitable, when Ann suddenly pulled back and laughed nervously. Beth, too, giggled a bit, and tried to think of something to say to fill the awkward silence. Ann said quickly, "I just want you to consider joining our guild!"

Both of them broke apart, turned back to the path and continued to walk, each silent in their thoughts. Beth couldn't believe what just happened. Rejected by a lesbian?!? She wasn't interested in Ann that way, but it still seemed a bit insulting that she had just been deemed unkissable!

He had been accepted to several schools, but with his dad so ill, Peter wanted to stay closer to home. He had been working through high school on his compressed music file idea and was itching to get some computer expert's opinions to overcome some major hurdles, but there weren't any in his small Ohio hometown of Spring. So he had decided to attend State U and it wouldn't take long to drive home if his mom needed him.

As an only child, he had been both smothered and left to raise himself, depending on the circumstance. He excelled in high school, and his good looks, slim physique, wavy blonde hair and bright blue eyes made him a chick magnet as soon as the local girls had decided boys weren't 'icky'. They didn't interest him a whole lot, though, as he had bigger fish to fry as he prepared to escape this little town with not much room for a future.

He had no problems getting dates. Parties, dates and school events were easy for him, but as soon a girl started to get clingy, he found himself backing away. He was too busy, anyway, working on his audio coding project. His mom encouraged him, and he had met often with the patent attorney a few towns over, even acquiring some early patents for his work.

Pete felt like he was perfectly suited for college life. He could do his own work, show up for classes, take part in dorm events, and mingle with others....but on his own terms. If he needed to hole himself up in his room and stare at his computer screen, nobody nagged him to get off, or to come down for dinner, or to be sociable. He signed up for every computer class he could, and picked his professors' brains about music parameters and compressions. But he seemed to be light years ahead of them, so he began working one on one with the department head. Little by little, the fog was lifting, and he felt ready to break through on his invention. Every spare minute, he met with his mentor and discussed psychoacoustics. Eventually, he was referred to the law department and was allowed to audit patent classes.

It was in his sophomore English class, near the end of the semester, when he looked up one snowy day and noticed a sparkling pair of eyes studying him. This girl had sat next to him many times, but he had barely noticed her. Until now. He and Ann began talking, and as they walked the quad together, they shared stories of their upbringing, hometowns, challenges, likes and dislikes. They both grew up as 'onlies', an only child with no siblings, and that gave them an instant connection.

They started meeting for coffee, then dinner, then began spending all their free time together. The more Pete got to know Ann, the more he realized she was for him. And the more Ann got to know Pete, she realized he was her soulmate.

They became inseparable and provided sounding boards to each other as they encountered problems in their courses, with friends, and pressures in life. He held her while she cried over the news of her little parakeet passing away. She comforted him when one of his early patent applications was flawed. They became an exclusive couple almost instantly, and Pete took Ann home to meet his parents. They, too, adored her. She had him meet her parents as well, and unbeknownst to her, Pete had taken her dad aside and asked his permission to wed his daughter. Beaming, the rotund man had shaken Pete's hand enthusiastically, and said yes. "But Ann follows her own mind," he insisted. "She'll have to approve you first!"

The following week, Pete dropped to his knee as they walked the quad together to class, completely stunning Ann as he proposed marriage. "But," he added, before she could answer, "We'll have to wait until I can support us. The final build of my audio compression tech is almost ready, and I should get a great price for it. Then you can pick out whatever engagement ring you'd like, I promise!" She helped him up, threw her arms around him, and almost shouted, "Yes!" Then she added, "You're such a nerd! And I love you!"

He loved how she was able to be supportive yet give him the space he needed. She was smart, and intuitive and warm and loving. He couldn't

43

wait until they were married. That gave him the edge to finish coding the digital audio sources, and he was ready to finalize his invention.

He and his attorney had made contact with Sony Music in New York City, and the company was very interested in his research and his earlier patents. Pete made another appointment with the patent attorney.

Against his better judgement, Stan had registered with an online dating site. He was sure he'd end up with some psycho woman who would stalk him, or key his car, or worse. But it had been a year since his divorce, and he finally felt ready to meet somebody. His friends had attempted a few half-hearted setups, and they had all ended up disasters. One did nothing but talk about her ex over coffee, another wasn't technically single, but separated....he sure didn't need some brawny weight lifter husband chasing him with a crowbar! And another gal he was set up with turned out to have so many tattoos and piercings, he was repulsed over dinner and couldn't eat! What kind of women do his friends think he likes?!?

So he chose a site he'd heard good things about, struggled with his profile description and photo, but ultimately got it done and uploaded. Stan was pleased to get a few nibbles, and he corresponded with a few until focusing on one woman called Ann2020. They'd graduated from messages through the site, to emails, to texts, and finally to phone calls. He was pretty sure this woman was worth starting a relationship with.

Her real name was Ann, and he learned her husband had died suddenly some time ago, she had one adult son who lived across the country, and she didn't work. He wanted to ask about that, wondering why she didn't have a job, but figured that would come up later. He had never heard of a woman that age (whatever it was; she'd only say she was very close to HIS age) who lost a spouse and didn't have to work.

Stan enjoyed his job and it paid very well. He just wanted somebody to share his life with. And he had already confirmed that this Ann had no piercings or tattoos, so he was pleased.

When it seemed from their phone conversations that they were ready to finally meet, he suggested Roshe's restaurant on McCord Rd about halfway between their homes. They decided to meet in the parking lot, as that restaurant could get very crowded. He asked what kind and color car she drove, so he could watch for her arrival. She didn't want to know his car, saying she wasn't very knowledgeable about cars, and that was fine with him. Stan sure didn't want an auto snob who coveted expensive cars, especially since he drove an old Ford Taurus.

The night finally arrived, and he chose a parking spot behind the restaurant near the outdoor patio. This way he had a full view of the traffic coming from her side of town and could look for her car. He had been nervous, so had gotten there ten minutes before the allotted time. He sat in his car, watching the oncoming cars. He thought he saw her, but the car that fit the description, driven by a woman that matched her profile pic, just sped on by. So he tried not to get his hopes up as the time clicked by.

Finally, Stan got out of the car, thinking maybe he had missed her arrival, and she could be parked up front. He walked around the building, passing the neatly manicured hedges, and stood by the front door. No car matching hers. He ducked inside the restaurant, made a quick rotation around the dining area, and came back outside.

Was she really going to stand him up? He couldn't believe it. She had seemed as into him as he was into her, and the thought of her standing him up had never crossed his mind. Just to be sure, he walked back around the building, this time going on the other side, past the dumpster and air conditioning unit, but returned to the patio near his car. Still no sign of her.

Shit. He had been so sure, so trusting. But he still shuffled around his car, watching the road, looking over his shoulder. No sign of her. After forty-five minutes beyond their chosen time, he gave up. Sighing, Stan got back in his car and drove out. No way was he going to contact her again….she had her chance, and she blew it!

Dear gramma,

Hope all's well with you, and that your lady friend is out of rehab and doing better. I know you've been so good about visiting her, but I'm sure all those visits are taking their toll on you! Don't over do, young lady, you have to stay healthy and happy for a long long time!

Yes, I'm thinking about doing something with Pete's workshop equipment. He loved going down the basement and 'making sawdust' as he called it. Pete was so talented, and I love all the furniture he made for us. He had a table saw, lathe, planer, mitre box, joiner, router, drill press ….ummmm….those are the names I can remember. They were pretty expensive, so somebody should be using them! Maybe I'll donate everything to the local community center. I know that a lot of men use the equipment there, so maybe someone would like to own the equipment themselves.

You asked about how I'm doing since Pete died. I know in my last letter, I was still a mess, but more time has gone by, and I'm coping fairly well now. I'm back to my regular routine of exercise classes, storytelling, quilting, line dancing and ukulele playing, plus all the rest. So I'm able to keep my mind busy, and I'm even thinking about dating again!

I hope that isn't scandalous to you, but I'd like to find someone to share my life with. It doesn't mean I'd love Pete's memory any less, but hey, I need to find somebody to kill the spiders for me…you know how they freak me out! Pete was always my hero bug squisher!

But it's not going too well. At my reenactor weekend, the guy I was performing with turned out to be married! And I had thought he had great possibilities! I can't stand a guy who lies about something like that, right? And I had really liked a man at my jam session group and I was hoping he'd ask me out, but I haven't seen him for a few months---I don't think he belongs any more. But the worst, was my experience on a dating site.

I know, I know, the whole idea just reeks of danger. But we had talked on the phone for weeks before we were to meet, and he really seemed like a great match. But then the night of our dinner date, he never showed up. I had been so nervous about the meeting, I drove right past the restaurant on the way there and had to turn around and come back! We were supposed to meet up in the parking lot, but when he wasn't there, I went inside, walked around, and he was nowhere. Made me mad! I even walked around the whole parking lot, past the rusty old heating equipment, through the patio, and then past the pretty bushes side, thinking I'd see him and we'd laugh about almost missing each other. But nope! I'm sure not giving him a second chance!

If you were here, you'd encourage me to try again, because I know, you're not a quitter! I didn't think I was, but maybe I'm just not going to find the right man second time around.

Anyway, I went to my yearly quilt retreat this weekend, the one I told you about on the phone last time we talked, the rustic one set back in the woods. I got loads of sewing done, met lots of new people, won some great prizes (yeah, MORE fabric, now I have MORE quilts to sew!! LOL) but I dunno, I didn't have as much fun as I have in the past.

Connor is very happy at his job and has had several promotions. He's so sweet and solicitous of me since his dad died. He spent two weeks here after that terrible day, and I feel kinda guilty he used vacation time for me, but he insisted I'm worth it. I miss him, living halfway across the country, but we talk all the time.

Be sure to let me know what colors your new living room has in it since you redecorated. I'll send you a pretty throw-sized quilt for cuddling up in on those cool evenings in front of the TV!

Love,

Ann

Ann parked her car outside the community center and went in. She knew where the wood shop was, from when she used to attend a quilt group here. She walked down the hall, saw the workshop and hesitated. Maybe she should go the office first. A sign on the door prohibited unauthorized persons from entering. She figured they'd be thrilled at the offer of free power tools, so this was authorized business.

She opened the door and walked into the beehive of activity. Saws buzzed, motors whined, and two men were hard at work 'making sawdust'. The smell of the wood shavings almost dissolved her resolve, remembering Pete. No, she told herself, you have to do this.

Ann gestured to the man closest to her, safety goggles in place, suggesting over the noise that he turn off his machine. It was so loud in there!

He looked up, saw her, reacting like he was slapped. "Hey, ma'am, you can't come in here. Didn't you see the sign?"

She started to explain she had, but this was a special case, as she was looking for someone who might want a donation of a workshop full of expensive tools.

He had already turned the table saw back on as she started explaining, not even giving her a chance. She continued listing the equipment she had, he glanced at her a few times, warily. She watched him work for a few minutes, wondering what she should do. She finished listing all the equipment, explaining how they were all well maintained and in perfect working order.

Bud was concentrating on routing the edges of the flag box; this was the third one he was making today. The office told him yesterday they had orders for five more, and not many men were willing to put in the time. He glanced over his shoulder and saw that the woman was still there, jabbering away. He couldn't hear anything through his earplugs. Finally, he punched the power button, and met her gaze. "What?"

"I know," she said, "It's hard to believe I'm giving it away. I don't want it to go to waste."

"What?" he repeated. "You're not supposed to be in here."

"I'm not doing this for the money, I can assure you. I'm just looking for a man who might be interested."

"Look lady, you'd better leave."

"But it's such a shame to have it all unused, don't you think? I'm serious, I really don't want any money. Please don't be suspicious."

He reached over and turned off the vacuum. "You gotta be kiddin' me! You're givin' it away?!" He had never met a hooker before, but he sure didn't expect them to look as classy as this lady.

She smiled so genuinely, he actually was impressed by her. But she ruined it by saying, "I'm serious. I'm not charging anything. Really. Are you interested?"

"No ma'am," he said firmly, "Nobody here is interested. We're busy, so you really have to go."

She continued as if she never heard him. "I know you're busy. But will you come over later? Can I give you my address?"

"No, I'm not coming over." Man, these broads were sure pushy!

"Will another man here do it?"

He raised an eyebrow. "No, lady, nobody here will do this with you."

She looked puzzled. "Nobody can use my equipment?"

"That's one way to put it," he snorted. "We're not interested, and you'd better go."

"Well," she asked louder over the piercing high-pitched whine of the other man's lathe. "Can you recommend another willing..." He cut her off, and took her arm, leading her to the door.

"Hey lady, this is not the time or the place for your very *generous* offer." He snickered as he emphasized the word 'generous'. He couldn't believe she had come in here looking for customers. Too classy a lady for this, he thought.

She continued to protest, pulling her arm away. "But I thought this was the perfect place: men who like to use their hands....what about that other gentleman, would he be interested?"

The brawny guy at the next work station finally noticed the visitor, turned off his machine, removed his earplugs and came over.

"What's going on, Bud? Doesn't she know she's not allowed in here?"

"Yeah, Mac, I told her. She doesn't care. She's hustling us..."

"No, no," Ann insisted. "I'm sincere. Do either of you own a pickup? You can come over now and...."

Mac interrupted her. "You like a pickup man, huh?" He leered.

"Well," she allowed, "There's more room in there, right? Don't be suspicious, I promise you, there's no strings attached. Totally free, no charge, no bills, no receipts. Think of the fun you'll have!"

The two men exchanged incredulous glances.

She continued. "Maybe you two would like to share? There's enough to go around for both of you!" She smiled.

51

Mac took her arm this time and moved her closer to the door. "I can't believe you, lady!"

"You mean if I were charging you for it, you'd appreciate the value THEN, and agree to accept it?!"

His eyes widened, and both men advanced toward her. "Now, do we have to call security?" Beat it!"

Ann glared. "You don't have to be rude! I just thought since I'm giving it away, you'd be happy to have it. If you already have this at home, you could just say so…."

Mac slammed the door behind her, drowning out her final words.

Tools Matter!

Posted: June 5, 2018 10:15 AM EDT

So many yard signs these days reference how people matter. Of course they do. And so do your quilting tools! So here is a reminder to give your favorite notions some attention as well.

Examine your seam ripper. Once the point is dull, bent or nicked, replace it. The curved part loses its thread cutting ability, so that part doesn't work as well, either. And even though we love the feel of a crisp, sharp rotary cutter blade, we're all guilty of continuing to use the old ones long past their prime. Even our favorite scissors can live on too long! Either get them sharpened or treat yourself to a new pair.

When we hear that our sewing machine needles should be replaced with each project or after sewing six to eight hours, many of us laugh.....we replace the needle when it breaks. No, no, no, my dears....think of the stress these needles endure and how our machines depend on them for a quality stitch. Replace that needle NOW!

Also take a look at your favorite ruler. You know, the one you use all the time, and drop every month or so! As your rotary blade runs along the edge, over time, it can shave off tiny bits. And rough handling or dropping the ruler can chip the corners. This affects their accuracy; they don't last forever!

Treat yourself to some replacement tools and/or parts; you'll be glad you did!

On the other hand, take a moment to appreciate the tools you have. The templates you used when you first began quilting. The marking pens that sketched out designs on so many projects; they're getting dry. Repurpose those and toss them into the grandchildren crafts box.

Do you own an old strip cutter set, from when they first came out? We all thought it was so cool to insert our new rotary cutters into the slots, to speed cut strips! Nobody knew those were just the precursors to today's more modern tools and shortcuts. Maybe it's time to revisit those old tools and find new current projects to use them on! Maybe we shouldn't be too quick to get rid of old familiar friends....

Perhaps you can point to the scraps from the first piece of fabric you ever bought! If you can do that, it's time to use that baby up!

Plan a scrap quilt now: begin sewing together those little bits in your scrap boxes, log cabin style. Start with an odd shape or a square, sew chunks around it, building outward and press when you have about six or seven parts sewn. Keep chain sewing, work on a bunch of chunks at a time, combine when you can, and eventually, slap your 12 ½" square ruler on it, and cut around....voila....a scrap block! What you cut off around it can begin another block. When you have twelve or sixteen blocks, sash them with leftover strips, add cornerstones, and you have a quilt that cost you nothing!

Reduce, reuse, recycle....I'm thinking a lot about that these days. Some things deserve that treatment, and some don't. Sometimes it's too tempting to just make a clean sweep in your life. But don't be too hasty. Consider the consequences. What are YOU thinking about tossing, reusing, replacing or donating?

~Ann

Hey, you free tomorrow afternoon?

Why?

I'm going to the community
center to play euchre. Ya know, Ann, I
told you about that. You've given me
excuses every time I ask.

I'm free. Not sure I wanna
go, it's been a long time since
I've played. Used to be
really good, tho.

I'm sure you're still good. And hey,
you might meet a nice man!

Debby, Debby, Debby
....you're killin' me.
I haven't exactly been tearing
up the world of romance,
considering the men I've
been meeting lately.

Fine. Just come and play.

What time again?

1:30

So, are everybody retirees
like you?!

LOL. Mostly. But everyone is
so nice.

See ya tomorrow.

55

Marcus logged off his computer, powered it off and packed up his messenger bag. He stopped at his secretary's desk and reminded her this was his afternoon for Kiwanis lunch and euchre at the community center. She checked her to-do list and promised him she'd have the papers done for Monday's closing.

He trotted to his car, reminding himself it had been too long since he worked out. Better swing by the health club tomorrow before work. He had a client who was close to making an offer on that Valley View Court property, and they were to meet at the house at 9 am. Plenty of time to hit the machine circuit, sweat off some pounds, shower and go close the deal.

The Kiwanis meeting would be shorter today, as there wasn't much business to discuss. Plus, the scheduled speaker didn't interest him, so he'd be able to make it to euchre on time. A good thing, too, because he had been dressed down by the seniors before for being late and holding up the game. Sheesh, if they're so desperate for players to round out the tables, you'd think they'd be happy to see him, no matter when he got there!

He pulled into the Red Parrot parking lot and took his regular spot in the last row. Might as well get some exercise walking the parking lot, Marcus told himself. Gotta work off this gut. The sting of coming to this restaurant was finally lessening, as this had been his wife's favorite dinner spot. For months now, he'd stop inside the front vestibule and be transported back in time as his Eileen would joke with the maître d' there. She and this host guy had been high school buddies, and she had gotten such a kick out of discovering him working there, she insisted they go there regularly. That was before she had gotten sick.

He unconsciously shook his head to clear out the memories of Eileen's diagnosis and rapid decline. How he had been caregiver for such a short time before she had passed away in his arms. They had been married for ten years, were passionate lovers and best friends. He had to stop himself from dwelling on the past. Anyway, that host guy didn't work there any more, which was good, as Marcus couldn't take the guy's continued solicitous inquiries about Eileen. Now, this restaurant represented Kiwanis meetings, and nothing more.

He went into the meeting room, checked in at the registration table, picked up a menu, and sat down at his regular spot. He was happy the server appeared at his side immediately. He ordered his usual chicken breast sandwich, no mayo, seasoned fries and fruit cup. Black coffee. Everyone chatted amiably before the food arrived. The president was sitting a few seats over, and Marcus gave him the answers to the food drive venue questions he had been assigned to investigate. Good. Now he didn't need to stay for the meeting at all.

He finished eating, chatting with the others, and the servers were clearing away the dirty dishes. So he said his goodbyes and trotted back to his car. Someday, he thought to himself, this parking lot jogging is gonna get him into trouble....someone will think he robbed the place and he's hightailing it outa there. He smiled at his little joke as he drove the few miles over to the community center. He parked, walked normally this time, and entered the building.

Marcus walked past the woodshop wistfully, wishing he had the power tools and the time to make things out of wood, like his dad had done. He got to the hall where the card players had assembled, and walked into the card room triumphantly, fifteen minutes early. Take THAT, old guys, he thought. You can't yell at me NOW!

He looked around the room and the many stark metal card tables and folding chairs. If he could sell this Valley View house, he'd make enough from the double dipping (it was his listing, as well), that he could afford to donate a whole room full of classy game tables with padded chairs. He had seen centers with furniture like that, and it had simmered in the back of his mind. If he purchased and donated the entire room's worth of gear, they would name the room after him. That would be great marketing for his business!

He saw a few new faces, so he went over to greet the newcomers, shaking their hands, passing out business cards. So many seniors, playing cards in

57

the middle of the afternoon. So many houses that would eventually be for sale. If he could get even a quarter of the listings, he'd be sitting pretty. His frequent networking around the community seemed to pay off for him. Most businessmen joined community things just for what it could get them. But Marcus really enjoyed the activities, the people and the kinship, as well as the business potential. He had been nominated for the realtor Excellent Neighbor Award several times, and had won the Notable Service Medal twice. Realtor of the Year would be within his grasp eventually, he hoped. So he continued to network, chat people up and exhibit genuine interest in others.

It was time to begin, so he took a seat and started shuffling the cards. He looked up and saw an incredibly beautiful woman hesitantly walk in, as if she wasn't sure she was in the right place. She looked too young to be here. Another woman popped up and ran to greet her. Debby, he think she was called, a typical senior he encountered here. They hugged, and she ushered the young, gorgeous newcomer to a place at her table. He didn't know this new player but wanted to meet her. He didn't even care if she had a house for sale. Marcus made a mental note to introduce himself when he rotated to her table.

Unfortunately, it didn't happen until near the end of the afternoon. He was having a dismal run of bad luck all around. His cards were low and ugly, he was accused of reneging by a feisty octogenarian not once, but twice. Marcus wasn't a great player, but he knew how to follow suit, so took offense at being yelled at by that old man. Naturally, it was right as that guy was pointing his finger into Marcus' chest when the beautiful woman was heading his way. A nice change from the wrinkled, argumentative old folks who dominated this activity.

He started to rise, avoiding the wizened digit thrust his way, and turned to face the most beautiful brown eyes he had ever seen. But he barely got a glimpse, as her gaze flickered over his score sheet. She obviously saw the small numbers and thought twice about being his partner. So she did an about face and scooted into an available seat at the adjacent table.

Well, he thought, I can't blame her for not wanting to partner with a loser! I'll catch up with her when the match was over. It was only another fifteen minutes until the scores were official: he had tanked to about the lowest score that afternoon. But not THE lowest, or he could have won the booby prize they always awarded. Second lowest didn't get to make a self-effacing speech and gamely accept a little wrapped trinket. Just the top scorer and the bottom scorer were recognized.

Oh, well. He politely applauded for the winners, and got up, stretching his long legs, and looked around for that woman. Maybe she was free for dinner. But before he could lay eyes on her, his cell phone vibrated, and he snatched it out of his pocket. The client who was set to look at that McMansion tomorrow. He put the phone to his ear and slipped out to the hallway to take the call, praying the deal wasn't going sour.

He was deep in conversation with this client, speaking smoothly and reassuringly. Finally, he ascertained it was only a time change and not cause to mourn, when the mystery woman slipped past him and walked down the hallway with that lady Debby, arm in arm, chattering away. By the time he had checked his calendar and confirmed the time change, they were gone. Marcus couldn't shake the feeling that a major missed opportunity had just occurred, and he didn't mean career-wise.

Blog: Therefore I Quilt

Things Aren't Always What They Seem

Posted: Aug 4, 2018 11:44 PM EDT

Have you ever bought a quilt pattern, gotten it home, and eagerly opened it, ready to plan your next quilt? And then you read the pattern through, discovering with horror that it uses a technique you hate?! Maybe it's paper piecing, and you really dislike getting all those paper bits off with tweezers. Or perhaps it turned out to be applique. You've tried needle turn: took too long. Tried raw edge: too messy looking. So applique turned out to be a dirty word to you! Or maybe step two of the pattern is "Make 286 of this block", and you just aren't in the mood for a mind-numbing activity like this.

For whatever reason, what do you do when this happens? Returning the pattern probably isn't an option. You may have purchased it on a Shop Hop in a faraway city. Or it was Final Sale on the clearance rack. Do you grit your teeth and soldier on, hating the project from day one? You felt you paid good money for this, and you need to use it. Or do you toss the pattern on the free table at your quilt guild? Or stick an address label and a discounted price on it to sell at the next guild rummage sale? I sure hope you don't just throw the pattern in the garbage!

Things aren't always what they seem, and quilting reflects this. Not only patterns, but the new ruler-du-jour you bought for a specific purpose, that turned out to be more work than NOT using it. Or a quilt book that didn't get you excited once you started reading it. Or a sewing notion that wasn't much help.

How you handle the disappointment says a lot about you as a person. Don't let your distress ruin your day. Soldier through. Find a solution and move on. Maybe you decide to use water soluble paper for the paper piecing and soak the paper off. Or you could work a deal with a quilting buddy: she appliques your blocks, and you do the free motion quilting on her next quilt. There's always a constructive way to deal with what you didn't anticipate.

Of course, one wasted pattern isn't a life-crushing event. But apply this lesson to the bigger picture and see if this helps you in the grand scheme of life!

~Ann

It was the first Tuesday of the month, so it was escort day at Blossom Hospital. Steve really enjoyed this volunteer job with his buddy Darrell, plus Ann. They'd been doing this gig together on the first and third Tuesdays for many years now, and always sat together when they attended hospital events. Volunteer appreciation days, holiday parties and guild luncheons were always more enjoyable with close friends. Steve was lucky that his job was flexible enough that he had some mornings free. Helping patients at the local hospital find their ways to appointments, procedures and discharges seemed like a noble effort.

He had his salmon colored blazer on and was ready to get in his exercise for the day. He usually wore his step tracker and was always pleased to note at the end of his shift that he had logged almost 10,000 steps. A more positive result than sitting at his desk job for eight hours a day! One of these days he should join a gym and get in real workouts, but for now, this walking would have to do. And pushing a patient in a wheelchair for transport or discharge was also good exercise for him, so this position was a win-win.

He greeted the other blazer-clad escorts in surgical waiting and walked on to the escort desk where Darrell sat frowning at his cell phone. Ann was already on her way with a wheelchair for a discharge on the eighth floor, so the guys took the opportunity before their phone rang again to discuss her.

"I wonder if she's dating again yet?" mused Darrell. "I'm almost eighty, so not in her dating pool, but you might be perfect for her!"

"You think?" replied Steve. "Ann's husband's been gone for a while. It was such a shame what happened to him."

Darrell looked up from his phone. "Yeah, so sad. Not sure how old he was, but if he was close to her age, it was way too young to die."

"I think they met in college, so yeah, they must be close in age," shared Steve. "She confided in me a few weeks ago when you weren't here. She admitted she's thinking about getting back out there again."

"That musta perked you up. You thinking of asking her out, Steve?"

Steve paused a minute before answering. "You mean on a date? I'd be interested! You think I have a chance with her?"

Darrell replied, "Of course, on a date, you dork! You have as good a shot as anybody, so you might as well..." He stopped talking as they saw Ann approaching with the empty wheelchair, and they grinned at her.

"You guys look like the cat who swallowed the canary! Were you talking about me?" she teased.

"Yup," said Darrell. The phone rang. Steve snatched it off the cradle and learned that two of them were needed in Central Supply right away. Steve and Darrell jumped up, both a bit guilty for being so transparent.

It was a long walk from the reception area, so they continued their conversation about Ann. Steve was pleased that Darrell said he often saw her studying him when he wasn't looking, like she was assessing his worthiness or something.

"That's good enough for me," said Steve. "I'd love to have a shot at her before other guys beat me to her, so I'm gonna give this some serious thought. I'm not big on rejection, though. If she would shut me right down, I couldn't handle it.

"You have such a big ego, my man," Darrell replied. "That shouldn't hold you back!"

"But it does. I've had some really bad experiences with women, and I'm kinda gun-shy."

They reached Central Supply, and Darrell yanked open the door. Steve followed him in, and they found a harried clerk, who barked out instructions to them. They had to take the key he handed them, and go to the supply closet down the hall, next to Cardiology. Find the big box on the top shelf labeled ExStorpp. "Get it down," the clerk continued. "There's a ladder in there. It'll take the two of you to bring it back here. Bring it to me. Stat!" He saw the men's blank looks, and added softly, "Thanks."

They exited the supply area and went down the hall past Cardiology to the closet. Steve inserted the key and turned it. He pressed down on the handle, and the door opened inward. They entered and saw what a tight space it was. No ladder. The ExStorpp box was there alright, and it was big.

Darrell hesitated. "You think we should go look for a ladder?" He stepped out into the hall through the open closet door and looked around for a maintenance guy. Naturally, there was no one around.

"No," Steve said, "We can do it. That supply guy was in a hurry; it could take half an hour to track down a ladder."

They studied the layout and the surrounding boxes, strategizing how best to extract the box. Darrell reached up and hefted the bottom a bit to see how heavy it was. "It's not too bad," he said. "We can definitely do this."

They worked out a plan. Darrell would start to pull the carton out, and Steve would free the surrounding boxes to release it. Then he would grab the other end, and they would lower it down. Sounded good.

It went fine for the first step. But when Steve gently jiggled aside the box that was blocking it, a flimsy carton on top of that began to slip. He felt like they were in an I Love Lucy episode as boxes began tumbling down. It was almost in slow motion, like dominos, as things began falling, splitting open, and contents were exploding everywhere.

"Crap!" Darrell blurted. Steve was busy shaking stuff off his head, what looked like confetti or something, but he still was able to reach up and grab the box with his buddy and lower it down.

They surveyed the damage. Darrell immediately started shoving things back in their boxes, swearing a blue streak. But Steve felt something in his

64

eye and stopped. He attempted to step back but was blocked by the door. "Wait!" he shouted. He yanked his phone out of his blazer pocket, opened the camera and hit the button to use it as a mirror. He held it up to his eye, trying to see what was in there.

"What's the matter, Steve?"

"Something got in my eye. I can't see it. It's burning."

"Lemme see." Darrell said. They stood toe to toe and Steve held his lids open, as Darrell peered in. "It's kinda dark in here, get closer to the door." They shuffled as one to get into the hallway light.

"Ow! Ow! Can you see anything?"

"Yeah, it's a piece of confetti. That stupid box that fell had holiday decorations in it. Hold still. I think I can get it."

Darrell reached around to the back of Steve's head to steady him, and got his face really close to Steve. At that exact moment, with his other eye, Steve could see Ann start to walk past the closet, stop abruptly, peer in, gasp, and quickly take off, walking fast.

"Got it!" said Darrell triumphantly. Steve looked down at his friend's palm at the little mylar frill. It said Celebrate! "You think we should get you to Employee Health to have a nurse look at your eye?"

"No, no, it feels fine. But Ann just walked by. She saw us....she thinks....oh my God, she thought..."

"What?" Darrell was confused.

"It probably looked like we were kissing! Oh crap...oh, no...this is bad...."

"Oh c'mon, it couldn't have." Darrell turned around and tried to judge the view from the hallway. "So you're saying she thinks...."

"Let's get out of here. Let's grab the box and deliver it." Steve wanted to sink into the floor and not have to deal with this. "Do not EVER discuss this again. With Ann or anyone. Promise?" He grabbed the collar of Darrell's blazer. "Promise me, dude!!"

As Ann was losing weight, she had purchased various sizes and brands of undergarments, deciding which she liked best for her new shape. Now that she had reached her goal weight and hoped to stay there forever, it was time to buy a supply of her new, current size. She called Elaine, her quilting buddy, and they arranged a shopping date. Might as well make it fun!

Elaine and Ann had discovered each other at the quilt guild meeting many years ago, and realized they shared many interests besides quilting. Elaine's two children were in the grade ahead of and behind Ann's son Connor, so when the women got together for a 'play date', the kids did too. The husbands got along as well, so they also enjoyed dinners together as families. They had tried a few couples-night-out events, and those were fun too. The four of them would attend plays, go out for dinner, and once even tried one of those escape room experiences.

It was such a good fit, and it was assumed the two couples would be lifelong friends. When Pete had passed away so suddenly, Elaine and her husband mourned in shock along with Ann and everyone else who knew them. They tried family events again without Pete, but it just wasn't the same without there being two men to share conversation and 'manly things', as the ladies put it. So now, the women just socialized. Ann was sad she was no longer a couple, but just a single. Social dynamics were different now, but she was coping.

And so today, Elaine pulled into Ann's driveway and honked. Ann came out of the house and got into the passenger side. They had conferred on the phone when they set up this date and had decided on a restaurant where there would be low-cal options for Ann. Elaine was lucky to have the metabolism and body index that she could generally eat what she wanted without worrying about gaining weight.

They had a nice lunch and enjoyed happy conversation. Then Ann shared her frustration over striking out with men she considered dating. One had not shown up for their date, and one man she was considering turned out to be gay, a fact she had never known. Elaine was supportive of her friend and remained optimistic; she knew Ann was a phenomenal woman, and any man should be thrilled to receive her attention!

Then it was time for their errands. The women started at the local dry cleaners, where Elaine had two of her husband's suits to pick up. Then it was the library branch near their home. They both checked out a few novels and audiobooks. Next it was the chain department store they both preferred. They each chose a shopping cart and perused the aisles. It was fun commenting on the clothing styles, browsing through the shoe department, and Ann always wanted to try on hats. In the lingerie section, Ann found the multipacks of name brand panties she liked the best and picked up two four-packs from the rack.

When they both were finished, the ladies headed to the checkouts. Ann unloaded her cart first, and the clerk scanned each item. Then, holding the underwear packs, the woman frowned at her register readout.

"I'm sorry, ma'am, but there is a recall on these and I can't sell them to you."

"Wait, what?" Ann was surprised.

"They came up as a recall, and you're not permitted to buy them." The employee started to put the two packages in a bin under the counter.

Ann managed to snatch one back from her. "That's impossible! They were just hanging with the other panties. There must be some mix-up. Give me the other one, and I'll go to the service counter and get this cleared up."

"No," the clerk insisted, and she snatched the package back from Ann. "I cannot sell these to you. They've been recalled."

Elaine, who had been listening, incredulously, while she unloaded her items behind Ann, spoke up. "Ann, if there's something wrong with them, you wouldn't really want to put them on your body!"

"But these are the ones that I want, and they were just hanging with the other underwear," Ann said, to both Elaine and the clerk, who had hidden the packages away and was scanning the remaining items.

"I'm sorry, ma'am. These are recalled."

Defeated, Ann paid for her remaining purchases, accepted the plastic bags, and waited by the checkout lane for Elaine to pay for her items. When Elaine was done, the women walked out of the store, laughing but a bit mortified at the underwear tug-of-war that had just occurred. In the car, Ann searched on her phone for the underwear name, the year 2018, and the word 'recall', and scanned through the results. Nothing. There was no confirmation that this particular brand of underwear had been recalled.

"So I get punished because some stock clerk transposed some numbers or made a mistake? I'm not allowed to buy what I want?! This isn't fair!"

Elaine had the brilliant idea to stop at the competitor department store a few miles down the road and look for the product there. They arrived at the plaza, went in the store and made a beeline right for the underwear aisle. Sure enough, the same name brand packages were hanging with the other products. Ann saw there was only one four pack in her size, however. She searched through all the others hoping to find an errant package in the wrong place. No luck. Shrugging, she told Elaine she'd buy these and hope there would be more when they restocked.

At the checkout, the ladies held their breath when the clerk swiped the package UPC. Nothing. No drama. No recall. Ann paid, accepted her bag, and she and Elaine left the store, giggling.

"Who knew there would be controversy over buying underpants!" Ann summarized, as they buckled in and were ready to head for home.

At that moment, a large spider appeared on the dashboard right in front of the passenger side. Ann screamed. Elaine looked over and saw the spider, pulled a tissue from her purse and squished the intruder.

"You're my hero," said Ann. "I really freak out at spiders!"

Elaine tossed the tissue into the car trash can, pulled out of the parking spot and said "What drama we've had today!"

Pete was ecstatic when the final paperwork was signed and filed. It was a journey he had single-mindedly plodded through, keeping his eye on the prize. In later years, he would modestly explain he was just in the right place at the right time. But truth be told, he worked very hard to be in the right place and be done at the right time. Sony saw the value his perceptual audio coding process could bring to their next generation of portable music players. Once they realized that Pete's technology was far superior to their own, they happily bought the patents from him for a lot of money. A LOT of money. Enough money for financial security for life.

Then it was a whirlwind of financial advisor meetings, setting up investments with an income flow, and all the monetary decisions he never thought he'd be dealing with at age 21. All the business meetings with Sony, attorneys, advisors and bankers consumed his schedule. He finally realized the smart thing to do was drop out of college and begin his real life. Working towards a degree at this time was pointless.

He wasn't sure if Ann was willing to do this too. He felt like her accepting his proposal was so hypothetical and distant for her, and they had never sketched out a timeline. Would she be willing to pick out rings and get married right away? Could she agree to quit school? And then immediately start a family? She had joked once that she never thought she'd be coming to school to get her MrS degree, which apparently was a baby boomer thing before women's liberation. He didn't know much about that, but he was sure that he wanted to wake up next to her every morning. In their shared bed, in their own home. With a baby slumbering down the hall in the nursery.

Maybe he WAS being sexist and trying to hold her down. If she wanted to get her degree, he would be willing to support her decision, doing whatever it took. Ann was the most important thing in his life now that his fortune was made and safe, with the future assured. He had to make sure she knew this.

They were meeting for dinner tonight after her late afternoon class. He waited until they had ordered and were holding hands, smiling happily at each other. He told her how the payment had been disbursed into holding and investment accounts, and all the paperwork was finally completed. Pete described to his fiancé how he had been advised to set up shell companies to handle his investments in real estate and sovereign wealth funds. He had had a crash course in finances, and now he explained all the details to Ann. Then he shared his vision for the future, and how he wanted his future to begin immediately. He held his breath when he finished with the part about resigning from university, buying wedding rings, getting married and buying a house. And while she stared at him, he added: and starting their family.

Ann wasn't usually speechless, as she was such an eloquent speaker. But a bunch of emotions ran through his mind, all of them scary, while she just looked at him. Would the marriage deal be off? Had he gone too far? She finally put down her fork, took her napkin off her lap, and folded it onto the table next to her plate. She looked deep into his eyes, smiled that million dollar smile of hers and said, "What are we waiting for? Let's go get married!"

The next week was a blur of activity, as they visited the bursar to withdraw from school, the jeweler to purchase their rings, and the courthouse to apply for the license. They learned with dismay that it would take five days for the license and could not marry until they had the license in hand. At least they didn't need any parental permission, as Ann was over the age of 18. But they were so busy while waiting, those five days just flew by.

They began working with a realtor looking for the perfect house. Pete and Ann wanted to stay near the university in case either of them wanted to resume their studies. Their real estate agent was among the best in the area, and when she learned they didn't need a mortgage and would be paying cash, she seemed to go into overdrive, scheduling showings one after another. The fifth house she showed them was perfect.

It was on a corner lot in a subdivision with lots of trees. Two stories with a full finished basement, the house was partial brick Tudor. 3800 square feet and with four bedrooms, it had lots of room for now and in the future. The first-floor laundry room was large and right off the attached 2 ½ car garage, plus there were 3 ½ baths. Ann quipped that was a lot of toilets for two people, but they both were thrilled at the prospect of growing into all that space. Even the kitchen seemed opulent, with granite countertops, gleaming white cabinets and timeless wood flooring. The current owners had recently replaced the 25-year-old original roof, and there was not one but two new furnaces that covered the different floors. The backyard was surrounded by a charming white picket fence, and a relatively new swing set was included with the house. All appliances were included, and the owners were moving out of state, wanting a quick sale.

Pete and Ann conferred while the realtor stepped outside to take a call. They decided to make an immediate offer at full asking price, contingent on satisfactory inspection. They would request a closing one week after that, with one-week possession thereafter. Ann looked slightly dazed, not totally understanding the realty jargon, and she just wanted to go look at the master bedroom again. She could just picture them in the attached bathroom suite, each at their own sink, with their own closets, and was excited at the prospect of living in such a lavish house.

It all went according to plan. They married at the courthouse one week later and closed on the house a week after that. Pete moved his stuff from his apartment, and Ann cleaned out her things from her dorm room. They went on a buying frenzy for a bed, furniture and tables. The thriftiness in Ann appeared, and she appealed to her new husband to approve her shopping for smaller items on 'the secondary market.' So they shopped resale shops, garage sales, consignment stores and church rummage sales. They picked up like-new dishes, silverware, small kitchen appliances, as well as lamps, coffee tables, file cabinets, desks and computer room furniture. Ann was tickled to find a brand-new cedar chest to place at the end of their bed which, if she had a trousseau, would have gone in there. She had a quilt started for their bed, so they bought linens and towels at department stores to match.

As they worked together furnishing the house, placing the items they'd purchased in each room, moving furniture around and getting everything perfect, they were so pleased. They would smile giddily at each other with happy satisfaction, working together towards a common goal: the rest of their lives.

Their parents were thrilled for them. They were appeased at the speediness of their matrimony by their promise to wed again in front of friends and family at some point in the future. The couple was young, in love, and had their whole lives ahead of them.

To: Betty <MommyOfAnn>
From: Ann <QuiltingFanatic>
Date: today

It has been an absolute zoo around here! I'm still escorting at the hospital, but I dunno, it doesn't seem as fun as it used to be. I know you told me to quit if I don't enjoy it, but I genuinely feel that I'm providing a valuable service to patients. Plus, I kinda think I'm paying it forward for the wonderful support I got when Pete was there. And it's reassuring to know I have a full-service hospital only five minutes from my home!

That's nice that Connor calls you now and then. He's such a sweet boy. I sorta wish he lived near me, but his talents would be wasted here. Hey, YOU adjusted to ME moving away, so I should be able to handle my baby boy living in California. Then again, you took off for Florida when dad retired, so we're living so far away from each other now. We should feel grateful for texts, email and cell phones, right? When you were first away from your family, long distance calls were expensive and a special occasion, right? I'm glad that's a thing of the past!

I recently played euchre at the community center…I hadn't played in a while, but I was surprised to see I still have that cutthroat edge I used to have at cards! I know winning isn't everything, but as dad used to say, "winning makes it a whole lot better!" Does he still say that?!?

I haven't decided what to do with Pete's workshop. I tried to donate it somewhere, but they were less than enthusiastic, which I don't quite understand. Maybe I'll learn to use all those tools! It's just like making quilts, but with wood instead of fabric, right?!

I tried a dating site and thought I found somebody, but it didn't happen. Perhaps I'll try again. The resurrectionist event was a hoot, and I really enjoyed it. I would consider joining a historic reenactment group, but frankly, there aren't enough hours in the day! My partner was nice, but he turned out to be married….so much for him.

And my annual quilt retreat was wonderful, as usual. Got lots of sewing done, won some great prizes and table favors, went off my diet at the tempting snack tables (but not too much!), but can't tell you much more than that. Remember: "what happens at quilt retreat, stays at quilt retreat!"

No, I don't go to that grieving support group any more. It really helped me in the beginning, but I think I'm finally ready to move on. It almost made me sadder to hear about other people's grief, losing children, babies, etc.

I'm totally immersed in my quilting now, and I am committed to donating quilts to charities every month. There are so many worthy groups: quilting missions traveling to areas where people have lost everything in tornados or hurricanes, children in foster care programs who have nothing, people with cancer who get cold during chemotherapy, even women who are escaping abusive husbands and move to a shelter with nothing but their children. You have taught me to always do what I can to make other people's lives better. Giving them warm, cuddly quilts is such a fun way to do it!

I'm getting much better on my ukulele now! Remember how I could only play three chords on that old thing you gave me when I was ten? Now that I bought a better instrument and go regularly to the uke jam sessions, I'm up to about 25 chords now! I hope to get good enough to incorporate music into my storytelling someday, but that might still be a long way off….I have a lot of improving to do!

You always suggest I'm overextending myself with all these groups I belong to. But remember, I live alone. This is my social life, all these activities. If I didn't have this sense of purpose each day, checking the calendar for where I need to be and what time, I'm not sure I could carry on without Pete.

Oh, I've reached my Forever status with Fat Busters now, so I have pledged to keep this weight off forever! I still weigh in regularly at the meetings. I'm thrilled to finally get down to pre-Connor weight again! I've made a gentleman friend there, and we've gone on this weight journey together for over two years now. I think I'm gonna invite him out for coffee after the meeting one of these days! Well, talk to ya soon. Tell dad I love him and wait until he sees his skinny little girl!

Love,
Ann

Blog: Therefore I Quilt

Deadlines? Or pressure?

Posted: Sept 15, 2018 08:46 AM EDT

Do you complete your sewing projects more effectively when you have a deadline? Maybe a guild challenge has you frantically cutting fabric at midnight. Or a baby shower this weekend forces you to throw on your walking foot and quilt that crib quilt. Or perhaps you're the type who sews the last stitches on your quilt binding one hour before the quilt is due at the quilt show. Don't despair! You're the kind of person who needs a fire lit under you to perform!

Or are you more of a leisurely quilter? You'll get around to it. There's always next week. You distract easily. Straightening your sewing area might reveal a lost tool, and forgetting your task, you immediately set to work using it. That's all okay, too!

But, you might choose to mix things up a bit. With no looming deadline nipping at your heels, give yourself permission to play a bit. Sew some fabric scraps together and see what develops. Experiment by changing up a pattern or a method. As yourself "What if....?" and answer the question to your satisfaction. If you're normally a laid-back sort of quilter, try working within some restraints, and see what happens. We grow in our craft when we shake ourselves out of a rut. Try it!

~Ann

Luke was consumed with grief. His darling wife, Patty, had passed away after a long battle with breast cancer. They had made the most of their last time together, and they knew the final day was coming, but that didn't mean it had any less sting when the day came.

His doctor had noticed during Luke's yearly checkup that his patient seemed lethargic, wasn't taking care of himself, and wasn't even taking his meds regularly. A lecture on the importance of administering thyroid and blood pressure pills habitually seemed to make no impact on his patient, so the doctor, who had been Patty and Luke's primary care physician for many years, took Luke aside at the checkout counter.

"I think you can benefit from a grief therapy group," he advised. "Many of my patients have attended and found them to have a positive impact on their healing." Luke took the paper the checkout clerk was holding out to him. "And please heed what we talked about. You need to take care of yourself."

The paper with the meeting location, schedule of times and days sat on the kitchen counter for a few weeks. Luke did better at showering, doing his laundry and taking his pills after the doctor's lecture, but he didn't feel like doing much else. He went to work, didn't talk to anyone, came home, turned on the TV, and zoned out until bedtime. He occasionally ate when he was hungry, but he couldn't bring himself to go back to his health club or find interest in reading or his online chess games. He had to look at his calendar now and then, if only to know when a weekend was coming up and he didn't have to go to work for a few days.

Finally his boss sidled up to him one afternoon. "Luke, I've been meaning to talk to you." Luke pushed back from his desk and stood up. "We've all noticed you haven't been the same since Patty passed away. I think you didn't take enough time to grieve after the funeral, so I talked to the HR department, and they suggest you take five weeks of personal time."

Luke squinted at his boss, Jason, a young pipsqueak who barged into their lives a year ago after the big merger. Half his age, this guy was usually only concerned with the bottom line, so a speech like this did not come easy to him, Luke knew. He cleared his throat. "And then what, sir?"

"And then we'll see how you're doing."

Luke felt panic rising in the back of his throat. Or bile. He couldn't be sure. "Are you saying my work has been substandard?"

Jason hesitated, put his hand on the older man's shoulder, and considered. "Ah, let's just say that I hope the time off will do you good. HR sent along this grief support group flyer for you, and I strongly suggest you attend these meetings."

Luke took the paper, slightly moist from Jason's sweaty palm, and shoved it in his pocket. "So I'm able to come back to work in five weeks?"

"Let's take things one step at a time. Go ahead and go home now. I'll call you in a few weeks and see how you're doing."

The traffic was light as Luke drove home, the phrase "one step at a time" reverberating in his head. He was used to rush hour traffic, so this commute felt odd. He parked in his driveway, let himself into the house, and flopped down on the couch. He flicked on the television, but a scan through the channels netted a foreign feeling, unaccustomed as he was to daytime TV shows. He shifted uneasily on the sofa, feeling the crackling of something in his pocket. He reached in and pulled out the flyer Jason had given him. He unfolded it, smoothed it out, and instantly recognized it as identical to the one that had been sitting on his counter for almost a month.

Maybe he should take this as a sign. He and Patty had always believed in karma, omens, and superstition. She even believed in past lives, and had even dabbled in a bit of witchcraft now and then. Maybe, he thought, these beliefs had given her comfort in her final days. She was sure she would be reborn after death, and sometimes confided to him facts about her previous lives. He admitted now that it would freak him out when they would go somewhere new, and she would share something like, "I've been here before." "No, you haven't," he would insist. "Yes, I have," she would protest. "I was wearing a black robe and purple boots, and I was carrying a jeweled scepter." He would shiver but say nothing.

If it was a sign, he'd better go to this meeting thing. He read the days and times and realized with a start there was a session in an hour. Luke felt a shiver run down his spine. Patty wanted him to go, he just knew it. He studied the little map at the bottom of the flyer and recognized the church at an intersection he passed by every day.

So, he went upstairs and opened his closet. He removed his shirt and tie, and chose a beige cable knit sweater that Patty had always liked on him. He hung his tie on the rack, noticed a few other ties crumpled on the floor under the rack, and thought maybe he'd pick them up. Another time. He threw his work shirt down the laundry chute and again made a note to himself that he should do laundry. Someday.

He went back downstairs and grabbed his keys from the counter. His gaze fell on the other flyer laying there, a bit pockmarked with frozen dinner splatters. Yup, the identical one. It's an omen.

He got back in his car, drove the few blocks to the church and parked. There were quite a few cars there. He went in the front door and squinted at the sign that greeted him in the vestibule. "Greif Group – Straight Ahead". Luke snorted. If they couldn't spell Grief right, maybe he shouldn't even be there. Patty had no patience for misspellings and punctuation errors. She even had a folder of clippings filed neatly in the cabinet above her desk. It was crammed full of mistakes she had found in newspapers, professional bulletins and magazines. She would show him each clipping as she found it, and they'd smile together, shaking their heads at the incompetence these days. The "it's / its" mistake was by far the most common; Patty could have had a separate folder just for that one.

Luke hadn't thought about that folder in a long time. Suddenly inspired, he realized he had to go home and look for it. He needed to pull the clippings out one-by-one and remember how Patty had showed it to him and they had

81

smiled. Yes, he had to go. This was an omen. A sign. He couldn't just ignore it. He turned and moved back towards the church door. Just as he reached it, it abruptly opened.

A woman stood there, confused at finding him there. "Are you the greeter?" she smiled up at him. "Er, no," Luke stammered, suddenly forgetting why he was standing there. "Um, I was just…" The woman touched his arm lightly. "You can show me where the grief group meets, thanks."

They walked together down the hall, heading towards the sound of voices. He felt slightly addled, trying to recall why he was walking with a beautiful woman down a strange hall towards a bunch of strangers. It was like a dream. He almost didn't want to wake up. Then he snapped back, and the reality of Patty gone, his job snatched out from under him, and a support group he had no interest in, hit him like a ton of bricks.

The two of them entered the room, and people were milling around, greeting each other and taking their seats in the circle of folding chairs. The woman and Luke sat down in two chairs next to each other, both looking around, one with great interest, and one slightly numb.

The leader spoke up, urging everyone to take their seats, and they'd begin. He explained that this was a judgement-free zone, and there was no set itinerary for grief; everyone experienced it differently. Some people nodded, and several people began speaking at once. The leader indicated which one had the floor.

The elderly woman explained the Kubler-Ross model of grief, developed by someone named Elisabeth Kubler-Ross. This psychiatrist had investigated a cycle in many grieving individuals and described grief as a five-stage process. Denial, anger, bargaining, depression and acceptance were the stages, and it could take days, weeks, months or even years for someone who is grieving to cycle through these emotions. Yet, some people didn't experience them all, or not in a certain order, and not all would be experienced the same way. This is all normal, she emphasized, and many attendees nodded sagely.

Then they all took turns, going around the circle, sharing their stories. An older man whose wife had just passed away. A young mother who lost a baby to sudden infant death syndrome. A twenty-something boy whose parents had both died in a car crash. Luke was horrified by all the sad stories and wondered how some of these people managed to get out of bed each morning. The woman he had walked in with shared how her 45-year-old husband had recently died suddenly. And then everybody was looking at him.

Luke cleared his throat. "I don't even want to be here." Several people said "Amen!" and "Me neither". He continued. "My wife Patty died two months ago of breast cancer. She fought the good fight for almost a year. We did everything right, followed all the doctors' orders, she had all the treatments, but it was a losing battle," he trailed off. "…and I just can't stand it…."

The man next to him told his experience with his adult daughter, then a couple shared their story of their eight-year-old son with leukemia. It went on and on. A lot of tissues, a lot of nose blowing. The leader took the floor again and spoke of how they were there to offer reassurance to each other, and how hope and healing were indeed possible.

Then people continued to share. The bereavement and grief were always present, but Luke was surprised there was also humor and laughter. Some began sharing the worst thing people had said to them after their losses, and there was a lot of nodding heads. Someone asked why major appliances in their house seemed to break within a month of their spouse dying. Another woman agreed, and said it was her furnace. Their fridge, another one said. It sounded weird, but apparently this really happened.

Luke thought this would be a meeting of palpable sadness, and in a way, it was. But there were uplifting words of wisdom, and he couldn't believe it when the leader stood up and announced that the ninety minutes was over, and they'd meet again on Saturday. And they were reminded that this Tuesday meeting was shorter, but on Saturdays, they had two hours.

He stood up, amazed that he had almost enjoyed the experience. Maybe 'enjoyed' wasn't the right word. But he was pleased that he wasn't the only one who felt so sad. No, he corrected his thoughts, 'pleased' wasn't the right word either. Maybe 'comforted'. Wait, did he just admit to himself that he felt comfort from this meeting? This thought boggled his mind.

He stood up and stretched, and Luke realized he felt like a single ray of sunshine had pierced through the gray cloud that had covered his world since the day Patty died. Just a sliver, though. He turned to the woman next to him. "Will I see you Saturday? I feel like we're the newcomers, and we have to stick together!" She smiled that radiant smile, and he noticed her amazing color flecked eyes. Was he really looking closely at another woman?!

And notice, he did, as the weeks flew by. He started tidying up his house, running the vacuum, dusting, reorganized his closet. It was hard bundling up Patty's clothing and dropping them off at the church, but he saw a poster advertising their upcoming rummage sale, so he figured someone else could enjoy the garments like his wife had. He looked forward to the twice weekly sessions, and he continued to sit next to that pretty lady each time. Luke began sharing more, and he had many private conversations with his lady friend before the meetings started. She was so nice, he even considered asking her for coffee after a meeting some time.

He got a haircut, bought some new clothes, shined his shoes. He started back at the health club, working out a little longer each time he went. His grief was still ever-present, but that little sliver of sunshine seemed to swell a bit more each week, and he felt like a new man. He kept attending the grief support group twice weekly. His leave from work was soon almost over, so he swung by the office and approached Jason's office one afternoon. Luke was whistling a happy lilt as he knocked and walked in. His boss looked up from his computer, and asked politely, "May I help you?" Then, "Oh, my God! Luke, is that you?" Luke smiled and nodded. "You look like a different man!" How ARE you?"

Jason jumped up and grabbed Luke's hand, pumping it in a handshake that seemed to go on forever. They talked for a long time, and Luke was pleased that he could start back to work on Monday morning. And Jason had even agreed to give him a few hours off each Tuesday morning to attend his grief group. "If this is what it does for you, you should never stop going!" Jason had said.

Luke went back to his old routine, but it was a 2.0 version, he shared in support group one day. No more TV dinners in front of the television. (The young people hadn't known what TV dinners were....ha!) He started going back to the local library, checking out and reading the latest novels, although he missed not being able to discuss them with Patty the way they used to. So he joined a book group at the library, and enjoyed those. He went back to his online chess games. He started going to the woodshop at the community center and helped them make flag boxes for veterans. He picked up poker again, although he hadn't played for years, and the group at his neighbor's house was a nice bunch of men. When it was his turn to host, he actually made a batch of brownies for the guys. They were amazed, even though he admitted it was from a mix. "But it was an expensive mix!" he said proudly.

He was whistling a happy tune when he walked down the hall to the church meeting room the next day. Wow, he thought to himself, could I really be feeling joy again? And I know in my heart this is not being untrue to Patty. She would want me to be happy again! Yup, he was going to ask that sweet lady out for coffee.

There was a different leader, he was surprised to see. It almost didn't seem like the same group with a different person in charge. This woman suggested they go around the circle first and say their first name, and why they were there. Luke had heard many of the members' stories before, but they had never shared names before, and it was odd to have each person identified. After he had said his name and told about Patty's death, it was his seatmate's turn, and he turned to look at her warmly, filled with resolve to ask her out and perhaps find love again.

85

"Hi, I'm Ann. I'm here because my husband died suddenly a few months ago, and I'm trying to get on with my life. But it's hard."

Luke stared, slack jawed. All he heard was Ann. He never knew. The rest of her words were like pesky buzzing flies in his ears. Ann. Ann! A shiver ran down his spine. Ann was Patty's middle name. Patricia Ann. Oh my God….this was a sign, an omen. He couldn't go out with this woman…Patty was letting him know she was watching, and she didn't want him to date anybody. Especially somebody named Ann!

Ann had resolved to clean up her quilting studio to survey the projects she had started, and today was the day. There was nothing on her schedule for today, so she promised herself to get it done.

She entered the room and looked around. It's amazing how much space there is in a bedroom when there's no double bed in there. But it didn't seem so large when there were unfinished projects, piles of fabric and notions on every surface. She figured she'd begin by emptying off the table in the center of the room, and she ran her hand along the painted wood surface as she walked across the studio.

Pete had made the table for her, and it was fabulous. She had wanted something that could be lowered so she could sit and quilt. That way it would hold her machine and the weight of the quilt as she manipulated it, quilting the layers together. And she wanted the table to be able to raise up so she could stand there when rotary cutting fabrics. It had to be at an ergonomic height to prevent back strain. She had read quilt magazine articles about setting up sewing studios, so she asked her husband if he could design something for her. She bought a commercial cutting mat that was 33 by 58 inches and provided him with the ideal heights that the experts recommended.

He had bought a hollow core hardwood door, trimmed it to fit the mat, and created sturdy legs for the table. In a Rube Goldberg-esque burst of inspiration, he rigged up pullies and ropes to raise and lower the table. He even included a lock pin she could use when the table was raised so it wouldn't come crashing down if she leaned on it too hard when cutting. Pete also thought ahead to when she wanted to take off the mat to store it during quilting, and he inserted thin dowels in a row under the table surface, so the mat could be slid in there and supported. Ann was convinced that man could do anything.

She began folding fabric, stashing it on the proper shelves in the closet. The bedroom had two large closets on one wall, with double bifold doors. There was lots of room when it was a clothes closet. So repurposing the closets with shelves provided a large amount of space for fabric, quilts, batting, unfinished projects, and more. Ann's extra sewing machines even fit in there.

She stacked her rulers on the bookshelf in the corner of the room that held her CD player. She enjoyed listening to audiobooks while in her studio. Pete had made that shelf for Connor's room when he needed more room for his toys. They had repurposed it years later in her studio when she needed more storage. The nightstands on either side of the daybed were handmade by him as well and had originally resided in the guest room. Even the set of drawers adjoining her sewing machine desk was made by Pete to her specifications. All her threads were in there, as well as her basting pins, and her rotary cutting, machine cleaning and iron accessories. She loved how he had made the front look like there were four drawers, but there were really just two extremely deep drawers. Seeing all his handiwork, all the things he had so lovingly made for her, Ann felt overwhelmed. She missed him so much.

Had Pete's touch really covered every part of this room? She opened the closet doors and surveyed the wire shelf racks he had bought to fit in there. The custom risers he had created to give double duty to the high built-in closet top shelves. Looking back to the daybed he had fashioned from Connor's twin mattress from when he was little, sitting lengthwise along the wall. She could sit there when planning and designing, and she had created a custom quilt to cover the bed. They had worked as a team designing this studio, and it was truly a labor of love.

Sighing, Ann tackled the piles on her sewing machine desk surface. Refolding, moving to their proper place, rotary cutting the smaller pieces into strips and stowing those in the plastic tubs for that purpose. Hmmm, the 2 ½" box was jam-packed. So was the miscellaneous scraps bin. It was time to plan a scrap quilt. That would be her next project. Just sew fabric bits together, adding strips and chunks, pressing it flat, and continuing to make it bigger. When her 12 ½" ruler would fit on it, she'd trim around the ruler, cut off the extra, save that part for the next block, and she'd have one beautiful quilt block. She would continue chain piecing the scraps; when she had twelve done, she would arrange them into three across and four down, then sew sashing strips and cornerstones between them. Then an outer border, and boom! A quilt top!

But for now, she'd better look over her UFO shelf, the UnFinished Objects she had started but abandoned. She pulled out the piles neatly tied up with fabric selvedge strips and laid them all out on the table. The disappearing pinwheel quilt made with hand dyed fabrics…it was so lovely, why exactly had she not finished it? Oh, there was the challenge for her quilt guild made with ugly fabric. Last January, anyone wanting to participate had to bring in a yard or more of their fabric they deemed ugly in a brown paper bag. Then, when all the bags were piled up at the meeting, everyone who brought one had to pick a bag. They all laughed as each person opened their bag and showed what they inherited. It sure proved that ugliness was in the eye of the beholder! Ann's bag had a stripe with very uncomplimentary colors. She had made a throw-sized top from a quilt magazine pattern and then stowed it away. The finished projects were due at the January meeting. Now she had just three months left to layer it with a backing and batting, quilt it, trim it, bind it and sew on a label….better do that one soon!

But look, here was the wool block-of-the-month wall hanging that still needed stitching around the little figures fused on the pieced squares. That was supposed to be done by Christmas for her neighbor, so she'd better get hopping on that, first! She picked up the partially finished bargellos made with juvenile fabric she'd be delivering to Project Linus when finished. That one could wait. So could the next one, the lanterns row quilt she had started a few years ago with her blue and white scraps. And the western quilt made with all her horse, scenery and bandana fabric; there was no deadline with that one. Or the modern quilt with the graphic blocks, still waiting to be sewn together. Or the half-square triangle project made from leftover pieces. And the snowballed blocks. And the log cabins. And the architectural quilt top that just needed borders, and the luscious florals with only half the blocks done. Yikes, there were way more UFOs in here than she had thought. She really needed to finish a few before starting any more projects!

But she looked longingly at the pile of quilt patterns she had recently purchased, picked up from the guild's free table, or torn out from quilt magazines. So many quilts, so little time! Ann lovingly replaced the bundles of unfinished projects, the shortest deadlines on top, and resolved to come back after lunch to sew.

It was Wednesday morning, so Roger skipped breakfast. He grabbed a low-calorie protein bar and headed out for his Fat Busters meeting. It worked out great that his photography job was so flexible, and he never scheduled appointments first thing Wednesdays so he could get his weekly dose of inspiration.

He had been heavy as long as he could remember. His parents considered him an adorable, plump toddler, so all his affectionate family nicknames reflected this: butterball, chubster, crisco kid, and dumpling. Those stuck for many years. Which wasn't really fair, he always thought; his whole family was on the heavy side. Family events always revolved around meals with heavy, fattening foods. Real cream, thick pasta dripping with butter, deep fried everything, fatty meats and cheeses, French fries and onion rings, potpies....he barely remembered ever eating vegetables. Or fruit. Except for apple pies and banana splits.

And his family had quite a history with desserts. They all ate dessert with every meal. Was it such a mystery that they all packed on the pounds? Rich cupcakes with mounds of frosting, sweet pies, thick oozing donuts, and oh, the cakes....he had such fond memories of those. Roger never met a cake he didn't like.

Food definitely represented love for Roger growing up, and his weight reflected that. In grade school, his mom bought him clothing in the 'husky' section of the department store. The names his classmates called him were not so sweet: porky, walrus, pudgy Roger, and worse. He regularly got into fistfights on the playground with his tormenters.

As a preteen, he joined a few team sports, and between practices and games, he started slimming down. But not much, as food continued to be a self-soothing escape for him. He was a decent student, but he found it hard to volunteer answers in class or speak in front of others. His favorite spot was fading into the background, which was why he discovered photography.

Behind the camera lens, he could be anonymous, nameless, part of the landscape. He joined the school camera club as well as the community photography group that met at the local library. It was actually there he made connections that served him well when it was time to find employment.

Roger began working as a photographer in earnest, taking portraits for the local studio, selling photos to magazines and websites, framing, displaying and selling his best shots at local restaurants and businesses. He found that he could really make money at this, which pleased him. By the time he graduated high school, he had made a name for himself, and it didn't involve his weight.

He began opening up to people, especially women. He found many like-minded women at his clubs and studios. He joined a gym and worked with a personal trainer. It was slow going. But it was there that he met Cindy. She, too, was trying to slim down and build muscle, and they had so much in common. They began going out for coffee after working out, which turned into real dates, and finally, they started getting serious.

When he had the confidence to propose, she said yes. They planned their wedding together. Cindy started a serious diet to fit into the wedding dress of her dreams. She had tried to include Roger in the new eating plans, but he was encountering stress in his career, as he lost several major gigs to his competitors, so weight loss was the least of his worries. She never fit into the size 6 dress she wanted, but he loved her as a size 14 anyway.

Their marriage had been great at first. She was a legal secretary at a major law firm downtown, and apparently, she was a good one, because she received many raises and promotions. Over the years, he would be gone numerous evenings and weekends photographing events, galas and weddings. Cindy worked during the day, but as the years went on, she had more and more late meetings, and they hardly ever saw each other.

It all blew up on their tenth wedding anniversary. He had been sure to avoid scheduling a shoot on that night so they could go out for a romantic dinner. Roger could hardly remember when they last had romance in their life, and he missed it. He made reservations at the fancy new restaurant that had recently opened ten minutes away. She had agreed to make the time, but as usual, she texted him she was running late for meetings and would meet him there. He arrived on time, sat at their table, perused the menu, ate a roll from the bread basket, drank both their waters, and still Cindy hadn't arrived. He played a few phone games, deflected the waiter's attention several times, and was starting to worry when she was over thirty minutes late.

Finally, she breezed in, sat down across from him, and without even saying hello, she launched into what must have been a well-rehearsed speech. They had grown apart, she wasn't happy, she had found someone else, she was filing for divorce. Roger could hardly comprehend what she was saying. Her steely resolve indicated no regret whatsoever, and he just sat there open mouthed.

Cindy stood up, said she had a date, and marched resolutely away from the table and out of the restaurant. Roger felt ill. He had been ready to wish her a happy anniversary, and now he had been warned to watch for the divorce papers.

The next months went by in a blur. Lawyers, meetings, negotiations, moving vans, final hearing, official signatures. Roger was now divorced, and it felt awful. It felt even worse when it was revealed that Cindy had been cheating on him for over two years with some man from her office. Roger was completely blindsided by that news. That guy was the 'someone else.' Roger really tried to bounce back from this, but it was hard. He gave himself pep talks and tried to maintain some normalcy in his life. He worked hard, he reactivated his gym membership, and he decided to work on his appearance. He decided to swing by that Fat Busters place he passed every day on the way to work. If he was going to be back in the game, he figured the first thing he should fix was his weight.

Those weekly meetings were like a breath of fresh air to him. To be around so many other like-minded people, all battling food addictions like him, was refreshing. Roger learned how to make wise decisions in the grocery store, and for the first time ever, he began reading the nutrition labels on the food he bought. The Fat Busters lecturer was really a nice lady. Shirley had started just like him, joining the group to lose weight, and after she was successful, she had been hired to work there. Now she inspired everyone to exercise more, eat healthier, and reward small victories in other ways than with food.

Wednesday mornings became the highlight of his week. There was always a pre-meeting meeting as people arrived, weighed in, and settled in their seats. People shared recipes, low calorie food ideas, and photos on their phones. Those who had attained their Forever status and no longer had to pay each week were especially inspiring. If they could lose the weight, maybe he could too!

Roger kept at it, recording what he ate, making better food choices, eating slower to appreciate every bite, walking more, and being mindful of things around him. He transitioned to lower calorie and healthier foods. He ate more fruits and vegetables and watched portion sizes. His weight began dropping, a pound, half a pound, two pounds, this was really working! He noticed that the same people came to the meeting each week, and he began learning their names. Dave was really nice; he had been coming for years now. He kept backsliding and didn't lose much weight, but he enjoyed the camaraderie of the group and kept coming....Roger really had to give him credit for that.

Mary served as the group's food reporter, checking grocery, warehouse and specialty stores for great tasting, low calorie snack foods that wouldn't bust their diets. She'd bring in the empty packages and pass them around so everyone could note the name or take photos with their phones so they'd remember. Bob seemed to be the globe trotter, flying all over the world for work. He'd tell tales of exotic foods he encountered in foreign restaurants, wondering how many calories they contained. These fellow Fat Busters were fascinating people! One lady experienced many calamities in her life and admitted to turning to food as an escape. Another lady had gained and lost the same fifty pounds many times in the past but resolved this time to lose it and keep it off. Everybody had a story to tell, and Roger really enjoyed listening to them.

Ann told about how she used line dancing as her exercise besides walking and aerobic classes and shared all the places she went to dance. Roger began sitting next to her and they talked before the meetings began. He truly liked her; she was extremely beautiful, with the loveliest eyes, brown flecked with green. He didn't even know eyes could be that color, and he was thinking how he'd like to photograph her face.

Ann had been attending for over two years now. She confided to him one day about her husband's sudden death and how it had set her weight loss journey back for a while, but she had finally reached her Forever status last week. Roger had missed that meeting and apologized for the appointment he hadn't been able to reschedule. He hugged her, and said he was sorry for not applauding for her and her success that day.

Wow, he thought, this woman was amazing. He had seen how she had shed so many pounds since he had first become aware of her, and she was so warm and welcoming to new members. To everybody, really. Even him! She always congratulated him for his recent weight loss, and she noticed how he was looking thinner, giving him encouragement. For the first time, he considered the possibility of seeing Ann outside of Fat Busters and wondered if he was worthy of someone like her. Hey, why not?

When the meeting was over, he bid his friends farewell, with an especially heartfelt goodbye to Ann. Her reaction seemed very enthusiastic, so he made up his mind that he would free up another hour next Wednesday and build in time for a coffee date with her. He'd try to make it very offhand and casual, to give her an out if she wasn't interested. But she had hugged him back today, so he had a feeling she might be receptive.

He gathered his weigh-in book and weekly newsletter and left quickly, peeling off his nametag, folding it in half and tossing it in the wastebasket by the door. He passed some latecomers coming in who had missed the meeting but still needed to weigh in. He trotted to his car, got settled, and he pulled out from his parking spot. He stopped the car abruptly as he saw someone familiar approaching the Fat Busters door. It was Cindy! His ex-wife. Cheating, conniving, life-destroying Cindy!! Roger couldn't believe it....she must have just joined last week when he wasn't there....he had never seen her there before. Crap! That sure ruined the whole thing for him; he'd have to find another location to go to now. There was no way he would sit in those meetings anywhere near Cindy. He'd miss Ann and all those other nice people, though. He fumed his whole way back to his office, resolving to look online for another Fat Busters location to attend.

Quilters' Halloween!

Posted: Oct 30, 2018 03:34 PM EDT

At this time of year, everyone thinks about ghosts, goblins and skeletons. We think there might be some in our sewing rooms. Have you noticed that your sewing machine might be haunted? Do the evil demons make your bobbin thread run out when you only have two more inches to sew? Do your decorative stitches mysteriously turn into zigzags?! (YOU sure didn't bump the stitch dial, right?)

Certainly you have poltergeists in your studio. They move your rotary cutter across the room, under the fabric. They also turn off your iron, and they turn your machine on when you <u>swear</u> you had turned it off. They also steal those little missing applique pieces.....

Ghost hunters find mysterious orbs of light as signs of spirits. Perhaps that's the explanation when your magnetic light falls off your machine and plops onto your needleplate. Or do your old marking pens leave marks that suddenly reappear on your quilt? Time for new markers....technology has improved, and there are lots to choose from!

And it must be goblins that cause your fabric to reproduce overnight....there's no way you really bought all that, right? The scraps, especially….you've sewed three scrap quilts, and your scrap bin is still overflowing!

Hmmmm……Happy Halloween!!

~Ann

Ann considered what she'd do about Halloween this year. In Connor's years of going trick or treating, Ann would stay home and pass out candy, while Pete would accompany his son to the neighborhood houses. In later years, Ann and Pete had performed porch scenes for the subdivision, dressing up and creating a different spooky tableau each year. Their last one had been the day before Pete died, and she could hardly believe that was the last one. If the two of them had known it would be their last day together, is that what they would have wanted to do? Knowing Pete, probably. He got such a kick out of planning and implementing the scenes. She would sew the costumes if they didn't have anything suitable, and the children in the area looked forward each Halloween to what new entertainment was in store for them.

She went down to the basement to find the cartons of Halloween costumes and accessories, and sighing, decided to lug them to the rec room ping pong table to sort through them. First she had to clean up her quilt basting supplies, laying all over the table. She gathered up the clamps first, stacking them in their basket. She used those to affix her quilt backings to the table, pulling them tight for layering with batting and the quilt top, so she could do the pin basting. The plastic box of safety pins went in the basket, too, along with the pointed dowels she used to protect her fingers while closing the pins.

Once the table was cleared, she began bringing the boxes out from the shelved area, one by one, and lined them up. The oldest boxes contained Connor's costumes from the early years. She held her breath for a moment and began pulling them out. Blueberry. M & M. Money bag. Ghostbuster. Those were the early days, when she could dress him up with what she envisioned. Then the newer ones, where he had input. Cowboy. Fireman. Monster. Doctor. The doctor costume was missing most components; she had borrowed those to use for one of their porch scenes. In Connor's later years, he either ripped up and ketchup-stained old jeans and shirts and trick-or-treated as a zombie or a hobo, or he stayed home and helped give out candy to the kids. She missed those days.

Sighing heavily, Ann considered asking Connor if he wanted any of these old costumes. But sensibility reigned, and she piled them into bags to give to Goodwill. Where were the porch scene items? The next boxes had decorations they used to adorn the house every October. The back end of a witch on a broom they attached on a tree. Light up pumpkins. Furry giant tarantulas. Happy Halloween banners they stuck on walls with rings of masking tape. Garlands of witch heads and pumpkins that lit up. Why was she keeping all this stuff?!

Finally she came to the giant plastic tub full of all the items she and Pete had used for their scenes. She pulled up a bar stool from the other end of the ping pong table and settled onto it to savor these items.

First up, the safari shirt, whip and monster mask. The safari helmet was missing, stowed with her storytelling accessories. Pete had rigged up a cage-like contraption with ropes on one end of the porch and paced behind it wearing all black and a mask, looking like a monster. She had worn the safari getup and carried a handmade whip. When the children stepped on the porch, their little voices trilling "Trick or Treat!", the actors went into action. She said she was a little busy restraining the monster she had just caught, but she would get them some candy. As she went over to the little tray table with the bucket of candy, she would turn her back to Pete, and he would reach through the 'bars' and grab her around the neck. She would scream (quite convincingly, she remembered!), and use her little whip to beat his arms away. Then she'd stagger to the children and looking dazed, give them their treats. The older children laughed and complimented the performance, but the younger ones stared, wide-eyed. For the really little kids, they would skip the attacking monster part.

These costumes had sat on the hallway floor for a week after Pete's death, so disheartened was Ann to even deal with them. She held the mask now in her hand, realizing her husband's face had been inside it on the last evening of his life. She turned the mask inside out, held it up to her own face and breathed deep. It smelled like rubber. She put it on the table with her safari gear.

Ann remembered how she'd keep track of how many children had visited each Halloween, first counting all the candy in the packages, and then counting what was left at the end of the night. Doing the math, she'd come up with a count of over 225 visitors. But it was never totally accurate and probably less, because she and Pete would sneak a few pieces throughout the evening!

The next accessories she came across were for the doctor scene, but some of the parts weren't there, either. Pete had reclined in a lounge chair from their patio, the carton of candy on his lap. Ann wore the bloody doctor costume with mask, medical gloves and headlamp. 'Blood-soaked' tools and implements littered the tray table, covered with a white towel. White sheets completely covered Pete and the treats, except for his head and bare feet. When children approached, Ann remembered how she'd say in a freakish voice, "Oh, you want candy? I'm in the middle of an operation right now! But if it's candy you want, I'll get you some!" Then she'd reach her gloved hand into the box of candy through the slit in the sheets, and Pete would writhe and wiggle his feet. She'd triumphantly carry the candy 'guts' over to the kids and pass them out. It was such an awesome illusion, it truly freaked them out. Pete really looked like he was prone on a table. She remembered how a parent, there with her children, had taken Ann aside after her children had tripped down the front walk running for the next house, and the woman complained, saying it was too scary!

Oh, here was the mad scientist scene items! That one was funny. Ann wore this blood-stained white lab coat, and Pete sat in a chair enclosed by a board with a circle cut out for his head. A tablecloth down to the ground covered the 'table', and in the dim light no one could see someone was sitting there. They had fashioned a dome covered with tin foil, and the 'platter' around Pete's head was embellished with fancy lettuce leaves. Her lines that year were "Oh, you want a treat? I'm a little busy right now, but here!" and she'd lift the lid and remove the pudding cups she had stacked around the disembodied head, and present one to each child. They'd gawk at Pete's pale face with black-rimmed eyes, and he'd move violently then to make sure they knew he was real! That usually got laughs instead of screams, but it was fun.

Another year they had recycled the same lab coat and cutout board illusion for Pete's head in a jar. Ann pulled from the bin the giant pretzel tub from the warehouse club, cut for his head to fit inside. The 'laboratory table' had weird looking tools and accessories, and she had just given the children their candy without a word. She remembered she'd had to keep reminding Pete to blink or open his mouth in a silent scream or some such movement, so people would know he was an actual person! That scene wasn't a favorite, and some of the older neighborhood kids had even said over their shoulder as they ran back down the sidewalk, "Last year's was better!"

Now she came to the two matching monster cavemen full head masks. They had both dressed alike in black shirts, pants, socks and shoes, and they sat side by side on the porch swing. The candy bowl was nestled between them, and the kids had to approach to get their treats. The fear lay in whether or not the 'monsters' would grab them. Which they didn't. She and Pete had argued about that detail, but she had insisted the anticipation and fear was better than any fast-scary motions.

The very bottom of the bin had the jester hat that she wore for the courtroom scene they performed one of their first Halloween tableaus. She had sat at a low table labeled '13th Circuit Court – Jester Judge presiding' and wore Connor's black high school graduation gown. Here was the court jester hat she had worn. She reached in the box again and pulled out the gavel and the base she banged it against that Pete had made in his workshop. Her script was even folded neatly with the props: "Here ye, here ye, this court is now in session. The Honorable Jester Judge presiding" she read. She recalled how most children were so intimidated, they forgot to say Trick or Treat, and she had to prompt them with "What say you?" Then she had turned to the 'jury' sitting on the porch swing. Pete was wearing a flannel shirt, blue jeans, straw hat and boots. He was sitting next to a dummy he had created by stuffing another flannel shirt and blue jeans with newspaper, attaching a pair of stuffed work gloves as hands. He had created feet with another pair of boots, put a second straw hat on the dummy's head, and the two of them wore funny matching moustaches. Ann found only one straw hat and remembered the other one was in with her storytelling stuff.

When prompted, Pete would pronounce the kids "Guilty" or he'd declare, "Hang 'em!" Then she'd would bang her gavel and announce, "I find you guilty in the first degree of begging, panhandling, mooching and soliciting, and hereby sentence you to take your punishment!" And then she'd hand the candy to the children. She and Pete always felt it was not their best scene, but they were still learning what was entertaining at that point. She remembered that most little children were so fascinated by the dummy, they had to be prompted to come get their treats!

Ann had emptied the tub now. It was so full of precious memories, though, so she loaded everything back in, got down from her stool and carried the bin back to the shelf. The other cartons with their items to donate, she carried upstairs to load into her trunk for delivering. As she turned out the basement lights, she gazed longingly at the old plastic bin holding all those Halloween memories. She whispered, "Happy Halloween, my sweet Peter. I love you." She closed the basement door behind her, deciding she had just celebrated Halloween in the best way possible, with the memories of her husband.

1993

Pete and Ann were very happy setting up housekeeping, establishing routines, and interacting with their friends and neighbors. They had settled near the university in case either wanted to return to school, but their lives were full and rewarding, and neither had any desire to rematriculate. Their life goal of having a family was quickly granted, as Ann got pregnant right away.

She chose an obstetrician with great care and took her scheduled checkups very seriously. She treated her pregnancy as if it were a job, reading every book the local library had on the subject. She could recite the size and development of the fetus at every step of gestation, knew all about the changes her body was undergoing, and felt totally prepared for labor and delivery. The couple lovingly decorated the nursery. They both kept in touch with their respective parents, and kept everyone updated on every tummy expansion, fluttery movements and cravings.

Ann was sure she would never have pregnancy cravings, but all she wanted was chocolate. It became a running joke that each bag of candy she brought home would be labeled 'baby food' by Pete, and Ann would consume the entire package in three or four days. Her doctor was monitoring her weight gain, and when she was in her second trimester, he would frown at the number the nurse would enter on Ann's computer record. But he still pronounced her healthy, while repeatedly stressing that too much weight gain would be hard to take off later.

Scans of her baby in utero were done, and they had debated whether or not they wanted to know the sex of their child. Curiosity won out, and it was revealed they were expecting a healthy baby boy. Research was done, names were suggested and discarded, and they finally tabled the name decision for now.

They attended labor and delivery classes at nearby Blossom Hospital, and Pete was an excellent coach. They signed up for baby care programs as well, as neither had ever helped care for a younger sibling, being the sole

104

child in their respective families. Ann felt confident and engaged, hoping that natural childbirth would be the plan for her. She contacted the local breast-feeding support group in case she should require any assistance.

So she felt quite prepared when she felt the first pangs of contractions before dinner one night. She waited a while before alerting Pete, to rule out false labor, but it sure seemed regular and genuine to her. They grinned at each other when she alerted him, she put away the dinner fixings she had just taken out of the fridge, and he fetched her suitcase that had been prepared and packed for a month now.

As he drove her to the hospital, Pete was happy and nervous, but a feeling of dread came over Ann. Everything had gone so well to this point; would something bad happen now? He tried to reassure her, and in the whirlwind of her admission and examination, she tried to calm herself. They settled into their private room on the eighth floor. No progress was made by midnight and labor seemed to have halted. The attending nurse reported that Ann's doctor had suggested she try to sleep, and they'd reevaluate in the morning. The room seemed quite cozy, but Ann thought it unlikely that she could fall asleep. The pull-out bed in the room was made up for Pete, and they both settled in.

Pete tossed and turned a while, listening to Ann. Finally, at around 2 am, he heard her soft, regular breathing that indicated she was asleep. He was starved, since he had skipped lunch that day and they never had dinner. He decided to go out to the nurses' station to see if they had anything he could eat. He learned they only had popsicles and Jello, so he was directed down to the ground floor where the cafeteria was located. He was told they had a skeleton crew at this time of night, but he'd be able to purchase some real food.

The elevator dinged as the door opened, and he stepped on. It occurred to him he should have some sort of beeper or something in case anything happened with his wife. All the way down to the lower level, he fretted that he didn't like leaving Ann alone. He resolved he'd grab a prepared sandwich, or whatever was quick, and return right away. He got off the elevator, looked for the sign indicating the cafeteria and headed that way.

The dark hallway was a bit spooky and he found the cafeteria was deserted. Most of their lights were dimmed as well. Pete found the cooler with yogurts, puddings, hummus and cracker cups, sandwiches and a few other things. He grabbed the first sandwich he saw and headed for the checkout. Nobody was there.

"Hello?" he called. Nothing. "Anybody here?" He walked back to where the food service counters were and called out again. No response. He definitely was feeling uneasy, and briefly wondered if he should just lay a five dollar bill on the counter and leave.

He shuffled back and forth a few more times, calling out to whomever was supposedly working. Just as he fished out a bill from his wallet and was ready to tuck it under something by the register, a breathless employee came out from the back.

"Sorry, I just had to run to the restroom. I'm here! What can I do for you?"

Pete glared at him, thinking, You can do your job, that's what you can do! I have a pregnant wife to get back to. But out loud, he just thrust his sandwich at the man with the five, said "I'll take this." He collected his change and a napkin and hustled back down the hall.

Again the elevator dinged, and the doors slid open. He ripped the plastic open and took a big bite of his sandwich. Mmmm, tuna. Again he was alone as he punched the button for the eighth floor, and chewing, he had an express ride all the way, with no stops. He exited and headed down the corridor. He saw a commotion down the hall and quickened his pace. Not their room, right?

But it was. Ann was sitting up in bed, panting, and she was surrounded by nurses. One ran past him out of the room. "What's happening? What's wrong??" They ignored him, and he tried to get closer to his wife. "What's going on?" he tried again. One nurse snapped off her latex gloves, and he noticed uneasily that it looked bloody.

"Everything's fine" that nurse responded. "Your baby decided now is a good time to arrive, so we're trying to get your doctor here."

"But…what if…how will she…?" Pete was sputtering, an icy chill running down his spine. He was finally able to get closer to the head of the bed, and locked eyes with Ann.

"Where were you?" she snapped. "I was awakened by somebody screaming down the hall, and I asked you if you heard it, and suddenly all these people were in here, and I don't know wha…."

"I'm here. I'm here," Pete interrupted. "I just ran out to get a sandwich. I'm sorry, Ann, I'm here now." He turned to the nurse. "What if her doctor doesn't get here?"

"The attending physician has been notified as well, so don't worry. This baby is coming now, and you need to back up, please."

There were orderlies, nurses and staff everywhere. Pete stepped back, and surprised himself by thinking, Where was all this help in the cafeteria?! He ran alongside the team as Ann's bed was quickly moved down the hall to the delivery room. She was panting and moaning and muttering how she needed to push. He suddenly snapped to attention that this was really happening, and he needed to remember what they had learned. What was he supposed to do? What? He couldn't think. Oh! Be reassuring and supportive, that was it! He looked down at his hand, where he still clutched the partially wrapped sandwich, and quickly jammed it in his pocket.

It was all so quick. Ann's doctor appeared, he made some quip about it being 3 am, Ann was draped and arranged for delivery, and she was told to push. Out came their son. Pete hadn't even gowned up yet! Someone slipped one over his arms and was tying it in the back just as the baby was held up for them to see. Wow! They watched as staff suctioned his little mouth and nose. The silence was deafening. Wasn't the baby supposed to cry? Time seemed to stand still. Pete detected the slightest scent of tuna fish coming from under his gown.

107

Just as Pete thought that, a small wail filled the room, and Ann started laughing from relief. They had done it…they had created a person! The baby was cleaned up, swaddled, and laid on Ann's chest. Pete and Ann looked at him, examining his face, marveling at his little hands, and then looked at each other. "Connor?" Ann asked. "Connor," Pete responded.

Pete was never able to eat tuna fish again.

Debby enjoyed having Ann and Pete as neighbors as soon as the young couple had moved in. She and her husband John had built their house when the development was under construction and had their pick of the lots. They had raised their family in that house, and now that John was gone, Debby remained there alone. Her adult daughters had urged her to downsize to a villa or condo, but she had no interest in that. She told them they could carry her out feet first when she passed away, but until then, she was happy living in her home.

When her oldest daughter was a teenager, she used to babysit for the little boy next door. Connor was a sweet child, never caused any problems, and Rebecca never had to frantically call her mother with a problem while she was watching him. Sometimes that had happened with other babysitting calamities in the neighborhood, like a wailing baby that wouldn't be soothed, or a blown fuse. Rebecca would just need to be talked through the emergency, and it always turned out fine. These experiences had served her well in preparation for raising her own family now, all these years later. But little Connor was always her favorite.

Debby got to know Ann and Pete quite well over the years and was quite sad to learn of Pete's sudden death. Now that Ann was a widow, albeit a young one, she and Debby had even more in common. Offspring living elsewhere, independent and financially secure, a large house and yard to care for alone, the two women often commiserated over their situations. They shared names and numbers of lawn care services, insurance agents, furnace and sprinkler maintenance companies, and entertainment options for single ladies. They often walked together as well.

Their neighborhood was walking distance to a lovely nearby 200 acre park with a large lake. Debby and Ann had measured together: from their houses to the park entrance, around the lake twice and home again, was exactly 3 miles. It took them about one hour, depending on whether or not they stopped to rest, admire nature, or hit the park restroom. The park was quite lovely, heavily wooded, with many water fowl and lots of park patrons enjoying nature. The spring was especially fun there, with duck couples raising their little babies, waddling behind them. Seeing the little goslings trailing behind the momma geese was charming as well, and the ladies enjoyed counting the babies. As the little ones grew, it got harder and harder to distinguish the offspring from the elders, as they all seemed the same size.

In the summer, park patrons were loud and raucous, swimming at the lake beach, the lifeguards blowing their whistles to maintain order. Families set up feasts at the picnic tables, and the charcoal grills scattered around the park grounds got lots of use. The "No Swimming" signs on the far end of the lake were often ignored by rebel teenagers, and Debby and Ann would cluck disapprovingly when they saw the rule breakers.

Surprisingly, winter was one of their favorite times of the year to walk the park. Large flagpoles would fly flags that reported the safety of the lake ice for skating or ice fishing. Red meant the lake was not frozen, or the ice too thin. Green indicated the ice core was deep enough to sustain the weight, and it was okay to walk, skate and fish through a hole people would cut out. The ladies always promised themselves they would walk all the way across the lake to the other side with a green flag. They'd bundle up, wear their best gripping snow boots, and step off the banks together onto the slippery surface. Their mittened hands would clutch each other for support and courage, but every time they tried it, one or the other would chicken out, and they'd return to the shore before they'd reach the halfway mark.

Winters at the park were not without drama. One year while walking, Debby and Ann noticed a crowd of people huddling at the lake's edge, intent on watching something. They went over to see what was going on. A deer must have wandered out on the unsteady ice. Near the middle of the lake, the animal had broken through and fallen into the icy water. To this day, the two women remembered watching with dismay as the exhausted deer swam in tiny circles, trying to keep its head above water. It couldn't get out and concerned citizens had found park employees to report the crisis. The good Samaritans were informed that nature had to take its course, as it was unsafe to attempt any rescue operation. People had been horrified. Survival of the fittest and all that, but it had been hard to watch.

But now it was autumn, another special time of year at the park. The many trees had begun their colorful display. Red, orange and yellow leaves began their fluttery descents to the ground, and the crisp piles of leaves would crackle under their feet as they followed the asphalt path around the still lake. By now the ducks and geese had started flying south in preparation for winter, heading for warmer climes.

Today, Debby and Ann seemed to have the park to themselves as they made their way around the lake. Their sneakers crunched through the accumulated leaves and they chatted away amiably. There was so much to discuss; they hadn't talked in a while. Debby shared stories of her grandchildren and their activities, the euchre matches she had won recently, and she asked how Ann's ukulele playing was coming along. Ann reported reaching her Fat Busters goal, and thanked her neighbor for furthering their exercise goals by walking together so much. The friends were just discussing whether they wanted to attend next month's fundraising banquet, when they crossed the back parking lot and walked under the canopy of trees by the playground.

Suddenly, they heard a loud rustling in the tree overhead. They instinctively stopped abruptly and looked up. The branches were swishing, and leaves were raining down. They watched curiously, and as they squinted upwards, a squirrel plummeted from the tree above them to the ground. Right in front of them! It scrambled onto its feet and ran off. The women watched it disappear into the bushes and looked at each other in amazement.

"Did a squirrel almost land on our heads?!?" Ann asked incredulously.

Debby was thunderstruck. When she found her voice, she said "It sure did!" They continued walking, looking over their shoulders a few times, not believing what they had seen. They laughed, agreeing that in the past, they had seen squirrels tightrope walking across telephone pole wires. So it was assumed that squirrels had excellent dexterity. What rodent couldn't hang on to a tree branch?!

As they rounded the curve and began their walk home, the women agreed this was a walk to remember. The thought briefly crossed Ann's mind that when she returned home, she would have run excitedly to tell the tale to Pete. But that was not an option now, and it made her sad.

I Spy….Memories?!?

Posted: Nov 6, 2018 08:31 AM EST

What do you see when you look at your scrap fabric? [You ARE saving your extra strips, half square triangles and scraps in an orderly fashion, right?!] When you sew them together for a scrap block, do you reminisce when you see certain prints?

Maybe that red and pink stripe is what you used on the nursery curtains, and you wonder how many years ago that was. That black metallic print was in the first quilt you made….yikes, why is that piece still around! Or the yellow polka dots on green….wasn't that little guy in the wall hanging you made in that class you took last year? And, oh, here's that strip of brown solid from last month's table runner….I'm so glad to use it all up, you think.

Our fabric stashes are trips down memory lane. You might still have that Daisy Kingdom print from the stuffed animal you were going to make before you discovered quilting. And the purple batik that's too beautiful to cut into still tempts you. And then there's the yardage of orange on beige that you can't believe you bought…what were you thinking?!

Embrace your reminiscences. Use your fabric, relish the memories, continue to appreciate where all those cotton bits originated. But don't believe the maxim "Whoever dies with the most fabric, wins." That is NOT true….USE your fabric, including yardage, pieces, scraps, and even selvedges. If you need some inspiration, stop into a quilt shop, look through quilt books and magazines, attend a quilt show. Heck, if you Google "quilt pattern", you'll get almost half a million hits! Browse around online ….you're sure to find ideas to inspire you!

~Ann

Hey, you gonna be at guild meeting
tomorrow night?

Yeah, I'm the auctioneer for
that Quilting/Shopping
Outside the Box Program.

I didn't know you're an auctioneer!

I'm not. I watched YouTube
videos and practiced. I'll
probably be pathetic, Elaine.

Oh, I don't think so.

Oh, yeah?

You can do anything you put your
mind to.   Are we carpooling?

Sure. I have a funny story to
tell you about my walk the
other day. And about a gig I
have at Kiwanis coming up.
Is it my turn to drive?

No, you drove last time when you
brought your suitcase of quilts
for show n tell, remember?

OK. Pick me up at 6:15? No
suitcase this time.

6:15 it is.

The church hall was abuzz with excited guild members. Over 125 people belonged to Quilters By The Way; it was the most vibrant, engaged quilting group, and had been in existence longer than other local groups. For over thirty years, like minded individuals who enjoyed the art of quilting met monthly to share their love of the craft. Other smaller newer groups had sprung up since, and some still existed, but many were a simple, 'everyone sit around the table and sew' format.

By The Way had endured, because dedicated volunteers made sure it did. They used membership fees to hire national speakers to entertain and instruct at their meetings. They held fundraisers, quilting destination bus trips, stash raffles, pot lucks and more to keep excitement levels high. Attendees were loyal, board members worked hard behind the scenes, and when nominating committees were tapped to find new officers, they were met with more Yeses than Nos. Program chairmen found creative, interesting ways to enlighten and engage the members, who were grateful for the inspiration at their meetings.

Ann had been an active member of the guild for many years and had held various board positions over time. Currently she was door prize chairman. She was responsible for providing a quilting prize that was awarded to one lucky member at each meeting. Everyone signed in on numbered sheets at the attendance table when they arrived, and during the evening, a box containing all the numbers was shaken up, and somebody pulled out the lucky number. Whoever had signed in on that number squealed with joy, and a beaming Ann hand delivered the goodies across the room to them. The guild had never provided a budget line item to fund purchase of door prizes, but members were very generous in donating new and gently used quilting-related things to the cause. As well, Ann regularly purchased clearance items she deemed desirable, or she would stumble on a garage sale with rock bottom prices on quilting related items. So her stockpile of prizes was grand, and members were always elated to be the winner.

As well, she was the charity reporter. As a condition of the church providing their hall and amenities to the guild, they wanted a yearly report of what charity endeavors members had participated in. People would

116

email, call or text Ann with their updates, or they would tell her or give her scraps of paper with their summaries at a meeting. Five quilts to Quilts of Compassion. Six baby kimonos to Baby University. Four lap quilts to a veterans' group. One pet bed to the local dog shelter. The pet beds were always fun…members would sew up a simple pillow case from their extra fabric yardage and throw all their washable scraps in there while sewing. Strips of batting, small pieces of fabric, bits of ribbon and thread. When it was three-quarters full, they would turn under the raw edges of the opening and machine stitch it closed. The shelters loved receiving these gifts. Really pretty ones, they would sell in their gift shops to fund the purchase of dog and cat foods. Others, they would provide to clients when they would adopt a stray. And quilters kept their scraps out of landfills….it was a win-win situation for all. One volunteer was in charge of loading into her car all the bed beds people brought to meetings, and she would make the rounds the next day of all the local shelters, delivering the beds. Ann did this job one year, and she loved the enthusiastic greetings she would get from the pet rescue employees.

She and Elaine sat together in the front row. They chatted amiably, but Ann kept popping up to take members' charity reports or answer people's questions about a quilting quandry they had. She didn't feel much like an expert, but her studio wall covered with quilt show blue ribbons said otherwise, and people treated her like a valuable resource.

The pile of pet beds by the door grew as more people arrived, excited at the prospect of tonight's program. The program chair had been explaining Quilting/Shopping Outside the Box for months now in the guild newsletters. They had never tried this event before, and nobody knew what to expect. Four creative members had been tapped to serve as shoppers and demonstrators. They were each given a budget of $25 and assigned a store type. One had dollar stores, one had hardware stores, another was assigned office supply stores, and one was shopping 'on the secondary market', that is, rummage and garage sales. They were to purchase items not necessarily intended for quilters, but what would be of use to quilters.

These ladies were to use these items however they liked, to show how they could be used. Whatever they sewed with them, as well as the leftover items in their packages, would be auctioned off that evening. Each would do their demos, then members would bid on and purchase (hopefully) everything. It was projected the money that came in that evening and the money that was spent by the four shoppers, would be equal. If the guild lost money, it would just be the cost of the program. If money was made, so much the better!

So anticipation was high as the program tables were prepared, and the meeting began. Not much guild business was required this evening, as nothing controversial required long debates or discussion. The president called for a report from the program chairman on the latest sew-in day, then the retreat committee got up to announce the dates of next year's retreat. A few more business items, then it was time for the 50/50 and fat quarter raffles. Throughout the early part of the evening, the raffle chairmen sold chances to split the money pot with the guild. Plus, those who donated a quarter yard chunk of fabric or purchased tickets could win all the accumulated fabric that evening. These were both great fundraisers for the guild and helped raise money to pay the mileage and lodging fees for out of town speakers who were booked to appear at the guild meetings.

Then Ann was called up to show the door prize. She held up a pretty floral tote bag, with the store tag still attached. She announced it contained two yards of flannel, a quilt pattern, a small pair of scissors, a pin cushion, and the hot new quilting novel everybody wanted to read. The value was $50! A number was drawn, and the sign-in sheet consulted. The lucky winner was thrilled to receive the gift Ann handed to her. And now it was time for the program.

The program chairman explained all four women would present their demos, then there would be a fifteen-minute break. Members could come up and examine the items, deciding what they wanted to bid on. There was time enough for bathroom breaks and more socializing. And then the auction would begin.

The first shopper went up to the front, and began unloading her bin of items, explaining what she had purchased from the hardware store. Small LED lights in a package of six would be great for sticking above our sewing machine beds for better illumination, and the lights would be sold individually. Picture hanging wire could be used for hanging our small wall quilts. She held up an exquisite wall hanging she had made that sported the wire at the top. A small purchased toilet brush could act as a remover of threads from our sewing room floors. More and more items came from her bin, receiving oohs and aahs.

Then the dollar store lady came up. She purchased packages of glue sticks, and had machine embroidered little holders for them so they wouldn't get lost. Inexpensive mugs, mason jars and goblets had become pin cushions. Small notebooks were embellished with fabric book covers, with ribbons as bookmarks. Little dollar scissors had been tucked into lovely holders hanging from ribbons to be worn around the neck. Tiny plastic boxes held glue sticks and ponytail holders to tame our thread spools. Sewing table organizers with little partitions held more glue sticks….those things became the running gag!

Next it was the secondary market shopper's turn. She had found like new hospital scrubs, shawls and swim trunks, and had cut them up, using the beautiful fabrics in tote bags, table runners, cosmetic bags and wall hangings. More and more gorgeous items were held up sewn with found fabrics, and members were incredulous that this lady had sewn up the contents of an expensive boutique!

Finally, the office supply store woman had her turn. She had purchased bubble wrap, using the plastic texture to stamp paint onto fabric. The wall hangings she made with that textured fabric were worthy of any art show. Murmuring was heard through the audience when they realized they could actually buy these exquisite art pieces! Then she showed how she had cut up plastic file folders into stencils, used a hobby knife to etch out patterns, and stamped paint through them onto fabric. The table runners and little zippered pouches she made with that fabric was breathtaking!

Wild applause completed the presentations, and the break was called. Members rushed up to inspect the tables full of items they could bring home, and the program chair looked visibly relieved. She had no idea how this program would pan out, but seeing the sheer quantity of items up for auction had extinguished her anxiety.

The room was abuzz with conversation and bursts of laughter. Now the announcement was made for everyone to take their seats. Ann took the microphone and was ready to begin. She had been practicing with auctioneer cadence, a skill she had never mastered before. She had appointed spotters to help her see bidders she might have missed, and a scribe to keep track of the winning bids. The guild treasurer sat at a table near the exit to collect payments. They were ready to begin.

Ann knew timing was everything. She decided to start with a few small things and work her way up to the valuable tote bags and wall hangings. Let the bidders get warmed up and see how this worked. Gosh, this was a responsibility! She took the little plastic boxes off the table and held them high.

"Okay, let's get started with a plastic lidded box containing one of these famous glue sticks. High bidder gets their choice of one, two or all three at that price. Who'll give me a quarter? Just one quarter. I've got it. Now fifty cents. Can I get fifty cents. Thank you. Now 75. I've got fifty, can I get 75. Looking for 75. I've got fifty, looking for 75. 75 anyone? Fifty going once, going twice, sold for fifty cents!"

She went over to the winner in the second row and asked how many she wanted. She held up three fingers. Ann said "High bidder takes all three," and the scribe scribbled on her paper. Ann went back to the front table, grabbed a mason jar pin cushion and began again. The cadence started getting easier, and she started speaking faster and faster, almost sounding like a real auctioneer. People laughed and bid and the merchandise was flying off the tables. It was funny when late bids would delay the auction, and Ann would quip that they'd be there all night.

It all went faster than they'd imagined, though, and the gorgeous tote bags, table runners and wall hangings were wildly popular. It seemed like everyone wanted to buy one, and the prices went higher and higher. Some sold for $25, some for $30, the most desirable pieces for $40 and up. Ann was getting a bit hoarse, and she looked at her watch when the last item was sold. Forty minutes….not bad!

Then it was show 'n tell time, and an array of gorgeous quilts were displayed for all to admire. Members began lining up at the treasurer's table, the scribe totaled her records, and it was obvious the program was a huge monetary success, a scenario no one had anticipated. The collected shopper expense receipts were a drop in the bucket compared to the money coming in. As people began leaving, they were commenting to the president that they should do this program again next year.

When Ann had accepted the speaking gig at Kiwanis, she never thought about the timing. Her auctioneering stint was the previous evening, and she hoped her hoarse voice would get back to normal in time for entertaining the luncheon crowd at Red Parrot restaurant. She had gargled with honey and apple cider vinegar, tried not to speak, and gotten lots of sleep, hoping to regain her normal, strong voice for the audience. It seemed to have worked, and as she pulled into the suburban restaurant's banquet hall parking lot, she voiced a few exploratory sentences. To her ears, she sounded normal, so all was well.

Their scheduling chairman had requested her storyteller brochure, and the day after she had emailed it to him, he had responded with his choice of programs. The Many Hats of Reading. Ann was pleased. It was one of her best presentations, and always a crowd pleaser. Years ago, she had participated in the library's summer reading program. There was a version for children, who had to come in to their local branch and present a little oral review of the books they read. Adults were offered a version just for them, writing their mini reviews of the books they read that summer on little entry sheets and depositing them into a box at their library branch. Drawings were held for prizes, and there were participant prizes as well. Nowadays, the whole program was run online, but 'in the old days,' pen and paper were the method.

At the end of the contest, Ann had an inspiration, and she asked if she could have all her entries returned to her. Luckily, the librarian still had them, and pulled all of the sheets with Ann's name for her to pick up. Ann had an idea for a storytelling program, and had looked over her titles, matching a hat, vest, scarf, mask, or other accessory for each book. She added in miscellaneous topics to round out the presentation, such as the value of reading aloud, how online dictionaries had replaced our old Funk & Wagnalls circa 1965, and some fun reading trivia. The section on dictionaries was quite interesting. Ann shared some of the new words that are added each year, and people really enjoyed that.

The Many Hats of Reading became her favorite storytelling performance. She had always enjoyed dressing up, and this gave her a chance to indulge her inner actress. It had evolved into an hour program, and it was funny, serious, entertaining and thought-provoking. She didn't perform any of her storytelling for children, but rather adults and seniors. She was tapped to perform at church groups, red hat ladies, reading clubs, professional associations, and more. Ann didn't even need to advertise any more. Word of mouth provided plenty of bookings, and she was proud to keep the gentle art of storytelling alive.

After the lovely luncheon, the Kiwanis president called up the scheduling chairman. He introduced Ann, and she went up to the dais. The large carton containing all her props sat on a chair on one side of her, a big empty bag on the chair on her other side. She started telling a bit about herself, telling the crowd she was a quilter, a hospital volunteer and a Fat Busters success story. She enjoyed jigsaw and crossword puzzles, played the ukulele, and loved to read. That led into the backstory on the library contest, and she began reading each book entry, one by one, with the accompanying accessory. She added little comments, jokes, and self-deprecating remarks. People smiled broadly, and the time flew by.

One by one, the visual aids came out of the box, she wore it, announced the book and author, then read the few sentences she had written for the contest. Then she'd dumped that item into the bag and select the next. The book "Tab Hunter Confidential" – a bright purple neck scarf, worn 1950s style. "Hawaii" by James Michener – a plastic Hawaiian lei. "When Will Jesus Bring the Park Chops?" by George Carlin – a clown wig. "Love, Alice" by Audrey Meadows of Honeymooners fame – an old fashioned apron Ann had sewn. "The Life and Times of the Thunderbolt Kid" by Bill Bryson – a cardboard thunderbolt she wore around her neck with elastic. "Fire on the Mountain" by John MacLean – Connor's old costume plastic fireman hat. "Animal Farm" – a straw hat. "Left Behind" by LaHaye & Jenkins – a piece of white netting plunked on her head. "The Last Dive" by Bernie Chowdhury – a pair of swim goggles. "John Glenn: A Memoir" – a caveman fur vest. That one always got a laugh. She'd quip, "Hey, I don't own a spacesuit!"

In between, Ann would pepper her speech with fun topics. She talked about how the Caldecott Award books were interesting to read from 1938 to present day, and how children's books had changed with the times. She read a list of old radio shows that predated television, and the seniors in the audience enjoyed reminiscing. She confided how her old tape player had crunched up a library audiotape and jammed. The punchline was: "The librarian said she wouldn't charge me for the tape if I didn't charge the library for my tape player. Of course, nowadays, those tapes are a thing of the past!"

She went on with more accessories paired with books: a Russian hat, Groucho glasses, a gold scarf, a bridesmaid hat, a bald headed mask, a head scarf, a silver beret, a witch hat. When she'd finished the book pairings, she reached into the box for a few more items and put them on and took them off in rapid succession: a coonskin cap, red velvet pimp fedora, Santa hat, tiara, and leather cap. She explained she had no books to match them with, but she just wanted to wear them! That always got appreciative laughs.

Then Ann reached into the almost empty box and brought out the final item. When she told the results of the library reading contest, and happily exclaimed she had won, she put on an oversized happy-face stovepipe hat and shared how she had won a pair of season's tickets to the library's lecture series featuring various authors, a value of $140.

The program over, she apologized for her unruly 'hat hair' from all the activity and asked for questions from the audience. Someone asked how she got started storytelling. She briefly told her tale of narrating band concerts when she was in grade school, performing in school plays in later years, and volunteering on the United Way Speakers Bureau as an adult. She learned the valuable lesson how one's voice could evoke strong emotions in other people, and she enjoyed the power of the spoken word. So she had hung her virtual shingle, developed a brochure, and accepted bookings, working within organizations' budgets. As a volunteer, getting a small stipend, or earning the big bucks, it was all good. That was met with hearty chuckles.

Another question was how she had accumulated all those hats and accessories. Ann admitted to loving dress up ever since she was little, plus, she loved the treasure hunt at garage sales. The light-up variety, the gaudy sequined hats, the leprechaun tams....she loved them all, and had never met a hat she didn't like!

A few book-specific questions followed, and the president finally had to cut off the questions, as time was up. Ann accepted her applause, and the meeting was adjourned. She dumped the overflowing bag and her notes into the box. She started back to her place at the table to retrieve her purse, and people began lining up to talk to her. She always loved when this happened. The stories people wanted to tell her confidentially could give her fodder for future storytelling topics. Anonymously, of course. She smiled at each comment, nodded at the stories, even if they were long and rambling. One after another luncheon attendees took their place before her, and suddenly, a familiar face appeared.

"Hi, Ann, I'm Marcus. From the Senior Center euchre group. I saw you there once with your friend Debby." He looked deep into her mesmerizing brown eyes, noticing now they had little flecks of green. He hadn't known that was possible.

"Oh, hi, Marcus. Yes, that was me. I don't get there very often." She searched her memory bank, trying to recall this man. It flashed before her eyes, something about pointed fingers, yelling, accusing someone of reneging. "Are you a reader?" she inquired politely.

He started answering, but she wasn't listening. He had been nasty, she remembered, picking fights with the old guys. Too bad, as he was quite handsome. She nodded absently at him, until she realized he was now talking about going out with her for coffee some time. She hadn't expected this, and hesitated, not sure what to say. He produced a business card, seemingly out of thin air, and forced it on her. "Give it some thought," he'd continued. "Give me a call. I'd love to get together!"

Ann stared politely at his perfectly coifed hair, slick business suit, the manicured fingers pressing the card on her. She reached out to take it and saw the realtor logo. Wonderful, she thought, as Marcus prattled on. A mean guy who wants me to list my house for sale. No thanks. She took the card and made a mental note to toss it into the nearest wastebasket.

Life was pretty good for Connor. He had no siblings to play with, but he didn't mind. He had a bunch of friends from school, neighborhood pals, and like-minded buddies from his various activities. His parents didn't hassle him too much and they were very generous when he wanted something. Connor's family life was quite different from that of his friends, as both his parents were almost always around. He learned to cook, bake and sew with his mom. He learned woodworking and electronics from his dad.

It was really cool having his dad around most of the time. He was very supportive and encouraged Connor's interest in how computers worked. They were both a bit scornful of how mom could never really understand what her husband had invented when in college, even though they both explained it to her all the time. Today's MP3s were around because of what his dad had created, and this 15-year-old was quite proud of his old man for being such a pioneer.

Every now and then, his dad would take Connor along with him to a seminar where he'd be speaking. Years ago, they had gone together to Germany, and that was cool. It didn't even matter they couldn't speak German; people spoke English to them, or there were translators. For a middle school kid to be able to travel to California, France and South Africa provided bragging rights for a long time after. Connor milked that as much as he could. But now, it was harder to get out of high school, and the timing of his dad's trips didn't coincide with his school vacations very often. Summers had been a good opportunity to travel, with lots of free time, but his friends were finding jobs mowing lawns, babysitting and doing landscape work around the neighborhood. They were all pressuring Connor to help out, and he found himself busy on their jobs, taking cuts of the income. That was nice, having his own money to buy video games his parents wouldn't approve of, and snacks at the mall food court.

Sometimes he'd go with his mom to her speaking engagements. He'd be mortified when she'd dress up with goofy hats and costumes. But he had to admit, she was pretty good at what she did, and people applauded for her at the end. And he liked that she was always making blankets. Er, quilts….his mom would get mad when he slipped and called them blankets. She had made the ones on his bed. When he was little, they had animals and letters and shapes, and then there was the Star Wars quilt, and now he slept under a Pirates of the Caribbean quilt. How the heck had she found Johnny Depp pirate fabric?! He had a feeling if he suddenly announced he was really into squids and octopuses, there'd be a squid/octopus quilt on his bed a month later! In fact, he had once told this thought to his mom, saying 'octopi' as the plural form, and she had corrected him.

School was pretty easy, and his dad was always riding the school principal that he should be in more advanced classes. The GATE program (Gifted and Talented Education) helped a little, but all Connor really wanted to learn was how computers and computer programs acted the way they did. The adults had wanted to skip Connor ahead a grade a few times in the past, but his mom had fought it. The school administration wanted to get his dad off their backs and move Connor up, his mom said. She didn't want her son to be the youngest in his classes. She felt that would put him at a disadvantage for the rest of his career and being a genius wouldn't matter. Connor didn't feel much like a genius, and certainly didn't want to be treated like one. So he had stayed on track with his school levels, and just never felt that his classes were hard. When he started studying for his learner's permit to prepare for getting a driving license, his mom had reminded him if he had skipped a few grades, he'd have been the only guy without a driver's license by graduation. So, he tried not to complain too much about his classes.

He was tall for his age and had inherited his parents' good looks. He was popular with the girls and that felt pretty good, but he didn't date much. He mostly hung out with his buddies at the mall, and sometimes the girls from school were there. They would squeal with delight when they saw him, and he would smile, pleased. But they always wanted to shop for jeans and clothes or look through the latest CDs in the music store. Connor wanted to hang around the computer store and pick the guys' brains. But his dad was smarter than they were, so that didn't hold much appeal.

He had begun zeroing in on what fascinated him most. When people would search something on their computers, they didn't give a thought to how or why that worked. Connor researched search engines. He learned Stanford students Sergey Brin and Larry Page developed a grad school project called BackRub, a search algorithm. Its name today was Google. He wanted to dig deeper on how companies appeared first in search results. His dad helped him a little, but mostly he puttered around on his own.

The guys in his grade were more interested in girls and sports. Connor liked those too, but he was more consumed with search engines. Maybe other guys considered him a nerd, but he didn't care. Those guys were just jerks.

BLOG: Therefore I Quilt

A Top Ten List!
Posted: Nov 13, 2018 02:04 PM EST

TOP TEN THINGS YOU WILL NEVER HEAR A QUILTER SAY:

10. Oh, that's OK, we don't need to stop at that 50% off fabric sale.

9. Why don't you dim the lights; I prefer to quilt when I can't see the fabric.

8. I hope everyone is bringing their husbands on the next quilt retreat.

7. Here, use my quilt to sunbathe on. Be sure to use plenty of oil.

6. I get all my projects done early.

5. What is a stash?

4.   Of course, we can sell one of my quilts to buy playoff tickets.

3. We don't need a lunch break, we can just sew for eight hours straight.

2. No power, no problem, I prefer to sew everything by hand.

And the number one thing you won't hear a quilter say?

1. Fabric? No thanks, I couldn't possibly ever want any more.

[thanks to Kathy Mathews of Quilting Sewing Creating]

~ Ann

Gary was looking forward to tonight's singles group meeting. His wife had passed away a few years ago, and it took him a long time to consider letting another woman into his life, but he was lonely. Connie had been ill for a long time, so she had prepared him well to be a widower. She had coached him on how to clean, cook, and shop in the most efficient ways possible. And he had listened and learned well. When Connie's time was finally up and she had softly passed away in his arms, he knew he'd be able to carry on.

And carry on he did. He had joined a grief therapy group and attended regularly after work. His job on the Jeep assembly line required massive concentration, so he was glad he had no time to dwell on his loneliness during the day. But evenings were hard. Eating dinner alone. Watching television alone. Getting ready for bed by himself. It was too much for him. He really needed to find a lady friend.

The grief group finally stopped helping him, and he was getting sick of telling his story meeting after meeting. The other peoples' stories were bringing him down, and he ultimately decided to stop going.

He started reading grocery store bulletin boards and newspaper "What's On" columns. He made a point of engaging his single co-workers in conversations on their breaks to learn how they met new people. Several of them talked about the singles group that met at the Elks club near the factory two evenings a week. Gary decided to attend and see what it was like.

He went home first to shower and change into a nice outfit. The burgundy brushed suede shirt that was Connie's favorite. His newest pair of chinos, with no stains. Yet. He carefully brushed his hair, trimmed his beard and moisturized his dry chapped hands. Hopefully he'd make an impression on some nice lady.

He chugged a beer before he left home to give him some courage. It had been a long time since he had made polite chit chat with women. He wasn't even sure if he could do it. As he drove to the hall where the group met, he ran some opening topics through his mind. Weather talk was lame. Sports talk probably wouldn't go over with women. Politics was dangerous. What possible icebreaker could he rely on?

Gary still hadn't decided by the time he steered his Jeep into a parking spot near the Elks entrance. He was a little early. There was time to stop by their bar for a quick one; he didn't know if there'd be drinks at the meeting. He didn't even know if it was run like the grief group....would they all sit in a circle and share their stories? He couldn't take that format again.

He sat at the bar and sipped his beer, trying to make it last until the scheduled start time. He checked his watch. Still ten minutes to go. He ordered a whiskey with a beer chaser this time. He resolved to come up with some conversation starters, and as he drank, he jotted down some ideas on a bar napkin. He stared up at the neon signs on the wall, lost in thought, downing his drinks. When he next looked down at his watch, Gary realized with a jolt that the event had started fifteen minutes ago.

He got down off his bar stool and wobbled a bit as he made his way down the hall. He realized he had left his napkin notes behind. No matter. He'd wing it. He pulled open the hall door and stepped inside, not believing his eyes. It was a party! There was a bar, and a song began playing, and couples were dancing. Clusters of people were sitting together and standing around the perimeter of the dance floor. Alright! This thing might work!

He walked around slowly, looking for familiar faces. Finally, he found a few guys from the assembly line, the ones who had told him about this singles group. He joined their little cluster, and there was good natured shoulder slapping and back pounding. He asked his buddies exactly how it worked meeting women there. All the men in the group began talking at once, and Gary did his best to follow. He caught a few phrases. Meat market. Divide and conquer. Go for the ugliest ones, they'd be the most grateful. He was horrified at what these guys were saying, and realized these men were not the ones he should be associating with.

He wandered over to the bar and bought a beer. He began mingling around the groups, with a hello here, and how ya doin' there. He swigged down the last of his drink and tossed the bottle into the recycling bin. Just then, he saw a beautiful woman standing alone near the door, as if she were trying to decide to enter or not. He decided it was now or never, and he approached her.

"Hi, there," he began. "I'm Gary, and this is my first time here. You too?"

The woman looked appreciative. "Yes. I was supposed to meet a friend, and she hasn't arrived yet."

"Well, let's wait together," he announced. Ha! He thought to himself, he'd never have guessed he could have come up with this intro!

She smiled, and he was dazzled by the radiance of her face. "I'm Ann. That's a good idea." They strolled together over to the bar, and he asked her what she'd like to drink. She looked over the choices and seemed undecided. "I'll just have a Diet Coke."

"Are you sure? Not a rum and Diet Coke?" he asked. She shook her head, and he ordered a Diet Coke for her and a beer for himself. He paid, and together they wandered over to the disc jockey and watched him for a while. Gary noticed his work buddies stealing glances over their shoulders at him, seeming incredulous at the beautiful companion who had chosen him.

They chatted amiably about how they had come to be there, and Ann confided this was her first time as well, and she briefly told the story of her husband's death. It turns out he had died about the same as Connie, and then it came out that both Ann and Gary had been at the Grief group at the same time as well.

"I'm surprised I didn't notice you," Gary exclaimed. "You're so beautiful!" She reddened slightly, and checked the door yet again, looking for her friend. They continued to chat, and he was pleased how easy she was to talk to.

Finally, he checked his watch and saw the party had been going on almost an hour and a half. "I don't think your friend is coming," he said. "What are you going to do?" Immediately he realized that was a dumb thing to say.

She looked around one more time and agreed she had been stood up. "I think I'd better go."

"No wait," he'd insisted. "This isn't a very good experience for you for your first time here. Let's go get a drink down the street at that nice, quiet restaurant with jazz trios. Do you like jazz?" He surprised himself at how that had come out of his mouth. He had never been to that place, had no idea if they had jazz, and felt like he was playing Cary Grant in an old movie.

"But…but I don't even know you." she said.

"Not true," he continued, surprising himself again. "We lost our spouses the same month, went to the same grief group and now the same singles group. You're Ann and I'm Gary. What more do we need to know?" He had concentrated on trying to enunciate carefully.

She paused, looked around one more time, seemed to be holding an internal debate, then looked him in the eyes and said, "Sure, let's go."

Ann walked ahead of him, and never saw him stumble slightly as he followed her out of the hall. He pointed out his car near the door, and suggested he drive to the bar down the street, and he'd return her to her car afterward. She hesitated slightly, then agreed. He walked around to the passenger door, gallantly opened it for her, and closed it carefully after she had settled in. He was grateful he had cleaned it out recently; he hadn't been expecting company.

She had never been in a Jeep before, and she asked lots of questions about it on the short drive. He parked, walked around to open her door, and she flashed that million dollar smile when she realized how she was being

134

treated like royalty. He opened the heavy wooden door into the restaurant, and took her elbow, ushering her in. They looked around in the foyer, deciding between the dining area or the bar.

"Let's just go to the bar," she said. "We won't be here long."

The hostess pointed to the bar and they swung onto stools by the door. He ordered himself a scotch and asked what Ann would like. "Um, I think I'll just stick with Diet Coke," she said. She told him how she had lost a lot of weight, and alcohol just wasn't worth the calories, as she'd rather have chocolate if she were going to indulge. He laughed, and they made easy conversation as they sipped their drinks.

Gary was just thinking how this Ann lady was a real knockout, and he'd love to see her again, when Ann drained her drink and announced she'd like to go back to the Elks and her car. Gary shrugged, drained his glass, and they got down off their stools. She descended so ladylike, and he dropped with an awkward thump, and she frowned. Keep it together, thought Gary. What would Cary Grant do?

He threw a twenty-dollar bill down on the bar and they walked out. Again he opened her door, and carefully closed it. He walked around to the driver side, and the walk seemed to take place underwater. He finally reached his door, opened it and got in. He started the car, pulled out of the spot, slightly nicking the concrete embankment with his rear wheel. He wobbled the car to the exit, looked both ways for traffic, then both ways again, and caught sight of Ann's horrified look.

He finally determined it was safe to pull out, and he drove in silence the two blocks down the street to the Elks. He asked where her car was, speaking slowly and carefully, trying to articulate each word. She pointed, he pulled in next to it, narrowly avoiding the rear bumper. She clutched her purse to her chest, opened the door herself, slammed it behind her, and called over her shoulder as she unlocked her door and got into her car. "Thanks, Gary. Goodnight."

135

He watched her go, waved feebly, and decided to go back inside the Elks for a nightcap. So much for her, he thought.

To: Betty <MommyOfAnn>
From: Ann <QuiltingFanatic>
Date: today

Hey, mom, how are things there? Did the podiatrist help you with those painful areas on your feet yet? How lucky for me that I inherited your bad feet....LOL....I've got a few spots that build up and start to hurt when I'm line dancing. I should call tomorrow and make an appointment. I need to get my teeth cleaned, too. Pete used to handle scheduling all those things, and I forget it's me that's supposed to be doing it now.

Connor's doing great. We talk every week. He has been worried about how I'm doing with Pete gone, but I keep assuring him I'm fine. He loves his work and has a large group of friends. He works out, belongs to various special interest groups like long distance biking. I really feel like he has grown up out there, since he started work so young.

Funny story: A squirrel fell out of a tree right in front of me and my friend at the park a while ago. Close enough to almost land on us! It's bad enough I have to worry about scary spiders...now I have to be concerned with dangerous squirrels?!?

My gig at Kiwanis went well, and they were a great audience. Remember I told you about learning how to be an auctioneer for my quilt guild's program? That went great, too, and the guild made a few hundred dollars on that event they were afraid they'd lose money on! I had practiced my syncopated rhythm a lot but doing it in person was a whole different ball game. The members were pretty forgiving, though; they knew I was an amateur. No, I don't plan on doing this professionally....I'm busy enough!

A guy came up to me after my Kiwanis speech, a man I had seen before at the senior center euchre group. I kinda remember him being in some altercation with another man over the cards. He's some realtor guy. He let me know he'd like to list my house for sale and forced his business card on me. Yuk. I hate those aggressive salesmen.

But even worse, listen to this. I went to that singles group party. Elaine was going to meet me there, but she was delayed coming back from something, I don't remember what. I met a nice man, and we had crossed paths before, so I agreed to go get a drink with him. He turned out to be an alcoholic! He drank like a fish, and I got into his car with him!! You don't have to lecture me, mom, I will never see him again, if I can help it. Another yuk!

So to summarize, men I'd consider dating either never show up again, or turn out to be scum. I sure realize now how lucky I was to have Pete for all those years...

Talk to ya soon.

As his senior year of high school was starting, Connor was still fascinated with Google searches, wondering why they acted the way they did. With his dad's help, he began experimenting with backlink breakdown, spending hours analyzing data, cross checking Google's search engine results page (SERP) with keyword queries. He started engaging value-added paradigms and was puzzled. Connor noticed a certain retailer's dominance in search results and suspected that Google's ranking system had serious flaws.

He checked and cross checked his results, and felt he was really on to something. He called his dad into his room and pointed to his computer screen. Connor explained what he suspected, that retailers could purchase their way to the top of SERPs fraudulently, tweaking the series of metrics that determined their relevance to the searched term. People searching for something generally clicked on the top search result, and a certain department store consistently appeared higher than the actual website for a specific item, like luggage. He wasn't sure Google was aware of this scam.

"You'd think they'd know, dad," Connor said. "But I don't think they know about this loophole. Can you help me get to somebody at Google?" His dad had a contact there and promised to get that employee's email address to him. After he did, Connor carefully prepared his message to that employee, and asked him to pass his concern on to the proper department. About a dozen email exchanges later with Google department heads, Connor's revealing discovery was the impetus for the famous New York Times article detailing the JCPenney search engine optimization incident. The store had purchased thousands of backlinks, often on dissimilar sites, and was able to dominate Google's SERPs over many queries involving clothing and other products. Their online sales rocketed. Indeed, Google had been unaware of this.

With Connor's name out there, reporters kept calling his home. Ann freaked out at all the attention, but Pete shrewdly looked for the positive spin. Over dinner one night at the height of the frenzy, he asked Connor if he would like to work for Google. The teen's eyes lit up, and they plotted out their strategies.

Google recognized Connor's input, and with some strategic emails and phone calls, Pete laid the groundwork for his son's dream. One week after Connor graduated high school, Google asked him to come to California to work for them, helping their team correct the flaws that existed within their ranking algorithm. It was an offer he couldn't refuse, so at eighteen years of age, Connor moved to Mountain View, California to work for Google.

True Confession Time!

Posted: Nov 20, 2018 07:04 AM EST

Are you obsessed with quilting? Do you find that cutting up fabric and then sewing it back together into warm and cuddly quilts is irresistible?

Maybe collecting fabric is your obsession. Perhaps your stash has grown to huge quantities. You love to buy fabric. You love to get fabric as a gift, or free from others who have too much. Maybe you inherit it, find it, discover more you didn't know you had. You wash it, iron it, fold it, stack it. You examine your fabric, consider which to use next, and move the piles around. You need more shelves, more closets, more table space, more time.

Or you love owning the latest gadgets. Notions. Rulers. Timesaving items. Automated cutters. Storage containers. The best scissors. Variegated threads. Seeing a new notion you've never seen before sets your heart aflutter. A new rotary cutter style? Gotta have it. A cutting system with slots for your cutter? Need it. Quilting ruler templates for your machine? Doesn't matter how much they are, you want the whole set.

Your sewing machine is humming. You're busy cutting, piecing, layering, quilting, binding and labeling. Quilting just may be your obsession; don't be ashamed to confess!

~Ann

Todd checked the daily log of scheduled patients and was pleased to see that Ann had an afternoon appointment. He had always liked chatting with her. She had been coming to the practice for many years now, and it was refreshing to trim up calluses and corns in a young beautiful woman. Most of his patients were seniors on Medicare with hammertoes, bunions and neuropathy. Performing surgery was lucrative enough, but regular visits from Ann were like a breath of fresh air. Her engaging smile that lit up her face, and those beautiful color flecked eyes unlike anything he had ever seen before meeting her….well, he thought, let's just say I'm looking forward to seeing her.

Her husband had passed away, Todd knew, from when Ann had updated her medical records. As a physician, he wasn't really supposed to notice those personal details, but Todd had a personal interest. He had been divorced for many years now, and always kept his mind open to new relationships.

It was a typical busy morning, and then Todd had a lunch date with Walter, the senior partner in the practice. They made polite conversation over their fettucine alfredo dishes, but Todd's mind was on Ann. There were no patients to see at hospital rounds today, so he went back to the office and took care of some paperwork until his first afternoon appointment.

Hammertoe. Then athlete's foot. The next door Todd entered held a smiling Ann, and she seemed to light up the room. God, that woman was exquisite. She explained she was attending a line dancing party soon and needed to be pain-free. He began trimming away her calluses with his scalpel and smiled when she reminded him not to make her bleed today, as she'd be on her feet for hours and hours. It was the cute way she said it: "Dr. White, be gentle with me today. I have major dance floor to cover and need my A-game!"

As he trimmed and pared, Ann confided she was thinking about entering the dating pool and was keeping her eyes open for new relationships.

"The men you consider had better be worthy of you, Ann. You're a very special lady and deserve the best!" As soon as it was out of his mouth, Todd thought to himself, what a dorky thing that was to say. She had laughed, then talked about her latest speaking gigs, and he didn't quite catch what she said about auctioneering; he noticed the callus formation on her right foot was more advanced than at her last visit.

Before she put her socks and shoes back on, they had the "surgery" talk, as she called it. He really could help correct those areas with surgery, but for years now, whenever he brought it up, she refused to discuss it. He was certainly willing to trim things up every few months for her instead, but she could not be convinced to consider permanent fixes. Personally, he was fine with this, as it gave him more chances to look into that lovely face on a regular basis.

And then, after discussing her uke playing and his guitar strumming, she was gone. He had considered saying something about making beautiful music together, but at least he had restrained himself. What the hell was wrong with him?! Every time he saw Ann, he fantasized about holding her in his arms. This could not go on.

He walked down the hall to Walter's office, and found him frowning at his computer screen.

"Have a minute?" Todd asked.

"Sure, what's up?"

"I was going to discuss this over lunch but thought it best to hold the discussion here."

A look of concern flickered across Walter's face. "You're not quitting to live the life of a rock star, are you?" He smiled tentatively.

"No, no," Todd hastened to defuse the situation. "I just wanted to review the office policy on fraternizing with patients. There's a single female

143

patient I would consider…that is, being a single man, I was thinking…."
He felt like a teenager standing before his father. This was not at all how
he wanted to handle this.

Walter held up his hands, stopping the young doctor from continuing.
"How long have you worked here, Todd? About five years, right?"

Todd nodded.

The elder physician continued. "The American Medical Association Code
of Medical Ethics Opinion 9 point one point one states that romantic or
sexual interactions between physicians and patients that occur concurrently
with the patient-physician relationship are unethical. Such interactions
detract from the goals of the patient-physician relationship and may exploit
the vulnerability of the patient, compromise the physician's ability to make
objective judgments about the patient's health care, and ultimately be
detrimental to the patient's well-being. A physician must terminate the
patient-physician relationship before initiating a dating, romantic, or sexual
relationship with a patient."

"Wow," Todd said. "Classic textbook quote. I'm impressed!"

"Yes," Walter smiled. "Not to mention, such relationships are expressively
prohibited as a term of your employment."

Todd nodded. "I understand."

Walter added, "And suggesting one of our patients secure treatment
elsewhere is not in our mission statement. Do you understand?"

"Yes, sir. Thank you for your time." Todd backed out of the room,
embarrassed by the entire conversation. Damn, he wished he had just kept
his mouth shut. So much for that idea, he thought, and went down the hall
to his next patient.

Dear Gramma:

I loved reading your letter about your redecorating escapades. You have more furniture stores where you are than I have here, so you're lucky to have so many choices. Your peach and gray throw quilt is almost done; I only have to sew on the binding. Then I'll pop it in the mail to you. Should be next week.

My blogging is still important to me. I know this whole concept is foreign to you...I can't even imagine NOT having a computer now, the way it was for you growing up! But my blog is a great outlet for writing about quilting and connecting with other quilters around the country and all over the world. People I'll never meet leave comments on my blog posts. That's how we connect, not talking on the phone, like you asked. I understand it's confusing. Imagine describing Velcro, televisions, cell phones, or walking on the moon to YOUR grandmother! Personally, I think all these inventions are wonderful improvements. I wonder what Connor's grandchild will be explaining to HIM someday that hadn't existed in his early days. Boggles the mind, imagining it!

Still keeping my weight off. I cheat every now and then, but my body's metabolism seems to have adjusted to the new me. I carry around my before/after photo in my purse and whip it out to inspire other people who ask me about losing the weight. I've enclosed the pic here. And knowing you're gonna ask, yes, you can show it to your friends! It's fun how I recreated the pose I used from when I was 54 pounds heavier, isn't it?!?

Sometimes, when I'm out somewhere, friends I haven't seen in a long time steal glances at me. They eventually come over to me and whisper, confidentially, "I see you've lost a lot of weight. Have you been sick?!" I laugh and share my Fat Busters story with them. I should get a cut from that organization, for all the people I've referred to them!

I've had lots of speaking gigs lately. Remember when you used to call me your little chatterbox when I was little? I love how your little chatterbox is now being paid to talk! I used to tell Pete he was lucky he got to hear me for free, but he'd just roll his eyes.

I've had a few mini-dates, like out for a drink, but they're not working out that great. The singles group didn't work out so hot for me either, but I'm going to revisit the online dating site again one of these days. I truly think the perfect companion is out there somewhere for me. Do YOU think so?

Call me when you get your quilt in the mail and tell me if you like it!

Love, Ann

Sewing Machine Tips!

Posted: Dec 4, 2018 08:17 AM EST

We sewists are proud to have mastered our power tools. That is, our sewing machines! Here are a few thoughts on how to better understand our equipment.

It's said that one section of thread moves back and forth through the needle and fabric sixty times before becoming a stitch. All the more reason to use high quality thread and to change needles frequently. So many of us have to admit we only change our machine needles when they break. But if you've ever seen a video of how a sewing machine operates, you can appreciate the stress a lowly little needle endures. Be good to your machine and change the needle before you start having problems! And a superior thread will perform better and won't lint nearly as much as cheaper threads.

Here's a secret if your machine is hard to thread. Never unthread it. Time to change thread? Cut it off at the spool and tie the new thread to the old with a box knot. Pull the knot through the entire system, pull gently through the needle, and you're all set! (Google the knot if you're not familiar, or use a square knot: right over left, left over right!)

Check the tension on your sewing machine: Put different color threads in top and bobbin. Sew a few inches. If bobbin color shows on top of fabric, loosen your tension by turning knob to a lower number. If the top thread shows on the bottom of the fabric, tighten tension to a higher number. If you don't know where to find your tension knob, look in your sewing machine manual.

Add a bobbin-empty indicator to your machine! Older sewing machines don't beep or flash when bobbin thread runs low. Use this trick for an easy indicator. Fill two bobbins with the same thread; use one as bobbin, other as top thread. When the top bobbin is getting low, so is the hidden one!

~Ann

The American Legion line dancers had been buzzing for weeks about the upcoming line dance party fundraiser, and Ann had been looking forward to it. Instead of lessons and music played on a computer, it was a country band with live music. It wasn't so much the band she was anticipating, but the opportunity to dance continually, with no interruption to walk through the dance steps first. Ann truly credited line dancing with helping her burn off calories and lose weight. This format of 'dancing the night away' was good for her weight maintenance. Plus, it would be fun!

She had heard that other line dancing groups came to the American Legion event from all the other communities. It would be fun to see what dances the other people had learned. Ann was a good enough dancer that, if she placed herself in the middle of the crowd, she could follow the other dancers' steps no matter which way they turned. Rae Jean was going to meet her there, and Doris, Susie, Rochelle, Marti and the others planned on being there too. Rochelle had been coaching Rae Jean with her turns and so she was getting much better now. Leanna seemed to remember every dance she had ever learned; Ann liked to position herself behind her for the best step cueing.

Rae Jean and Ann sat together in the dim light, watching people arrive. Rae Jean said it looked weird seeing the hall this way instead of brightly lit, the way it was on their instruction nights. Lani, Amy and Pat arrived, and sat down at their table. Ann wondered aloud why they never saw that nice guy from Tennessee…Joe…whatever had happened to him? Rae Jean mused she remembered seeing him leave early one night but didn't remember seeing him since.

The band finished tuning up and started playing, and Leanna counted out the beat at her table, thinking what dance could go with the song. She jumped up, went to the front of the dance floor and started the steps to Martini Time. The locals ran up to join her, and by the time the song was over, about 30 dancers were smiling and laughing on the floor. This was fun!

Dancers from the other areas were arriving, and they claimed tables of their own. Some of those groups wore matching shirts…how fun, thought Ann! It usually took a while before the different groups started socializing. Ann commented to her friends that it was like their old days of middle school dances, with the girls on one side and the boys on the other. The ladies smiled. Couples were two-stepping around the line dancers, staying on the outside to avoid collisions. There was Viv and her husband John; they waved as they danced past Ann. The canteen was busy, as people brought their drinks back to their tables, even buying whole pitchers of beer for their groups. Baskets of popcorn and shell-your-own-peanuts began appearing in the center of tables, and the sound level in the room was up a bunch of decibels.

Temperatures were rising, sweaters were shed, mini portable fans were pulled out of purses. Song after song, someone thought of what familiar dance would go with it, and they began leading the steps. A few songs had people a bit stumped, and it took a while until someone had an inspiration of what dance could fit the music. One song, they never thought of one until the last stanza began, and after one set of steps, it was over! They all had a laugh over that.

Slow songs brought out the couples, and the line dancers sat down to take a much-needed break. The couples either two-stepped over the floor, or danced the old-fashioned way, arms around each other, shuffling aimlessly, swaying to the music. It didn't matter, anything worked. It was at the start of one of the slow songs, and Ann was sitting with her friends, waiting for the tempo to pick up again, when she felt a tap on her shoulder.

"May I have this dance?" A handsome man was holding out his hand invitingly to her. Ann smiled, but felt unsure.

"I'm not very good at slow dances," she demurred.

"No problem," he assured her. "I'm very good at leading." She stood, and he took her hand, leading her out onto the dance floor.

He was right. He kept one hand at the small of her back, and she felt his firm pressure when it was time to change direction or step out. She was able to keep up fairly well, and they danced the whole dance together, then the next one, where he led off with a different dance. Ann had such a good time, and they grinned at each other each time they executed a fairly complicated mambo step in perfect synchronicity.

After that, a recognizable song was next, and as the line dancers reclaimed the dance floor, the stranger led Ann off the floor to his table on the other side of the room. "Will you sit this one out with me?" he asked.

"Sure, I need the break!" Ann replied. "Just let me get my purse." She walked quickly back to her table and grabbed her shoulder bag hanging from the chair next to Rae Jean. "I'll be over there," Ann pointed with her chin. Rae Jean had been checking her phone but looked up and in the direction her friend had indicated.

"Good choice," Ann's friend said.

It turns out the man's name was Andy, and he danced with a group in the next county. Ann didn't know that group, and promptly forgot the name. The two of them shared their stories, and they were instantly smitten with each other. Ann thought he was smart, funny, incredibly good looking, and so easy to talk to. They kept their conversation light and breezy, and then continued to dance every slow dance together. Andy got up to dance the line dances he knew, and Ann rejoined her friends when it was one they all did together. It was amusing how, sometimes, three different groups would be on different parts of the dance floor, dancing three different line dances to the same song. And it didn't matter, it was all fun, it all worked, and Ann was floating on air.

At one point near the end of the evening, Andy asked her to take out her cell phone. She pulled it from her purse's outer compartment, wondering why. He asked her to log in. She did so, and he indicated she should now give it to him. He must own the same model, Ann thought, because he instantly clicked on her phone app, opened her Contacts, clicked on New Contact, and entered his name and phone number. He clicked Save, closed Contacts, and gave the phone back to her.

"All you have to remember is the beginning of the alphabet," he quipped. "For Andy. Please call me. I'd like that."

The rest of the evening was a blur. Ann kept dancing, laughing with her friends, and chatting with Andy. Each time the band took a break, a volunteer had his computer set up and he acted like a disc jockey, playing familiar songs, calling out the dance. People kept on dancing and dancing. It was awesome. And the fevered crush of 125 people was a super successful fundraiser for the Legion, as well as a wonderful night for the attendees.

When the band finished up and the evening was over, Ann collected her purse and her coat and started saying her goodbyes to her friends. She looked for Andy to say goodnight, but he must have already left. She patted her phone in its compartment and thought to herself, I AM going to call that man!

The line dance party was officially over at 10:30 pm, but it was closer to 11 before everyone finished their socializing and finally went outside to their cars. Leanna, Susan and Dot had noticed the tall handsome man with Ann when they arrived and saw how he had so completely captivated their gal pal. Rae Jean didn't have much in the way of additional explanation, even though she had witnessed their meeting, so now they quizzed Ann to tell them who this mystery man was, where he was from, and was she going to see him again. Ann admitted she only knew his first name, couldn't remember the name of the dance group he belonged to, but he had given her his phone number. The gorgeous twosome had sparked much conversation during the evening among Ann's girlfriends, and all had agreed they looked like the perfect couple. The ladies told her so, and Ann blushed. She got some good-natured ribbing over their names: Ann and Andy. But they weren't raggedy!

These ladies had been friends with Ann while she was married to Pete, had been giving her emotional support while she mourned for him, and even now, still tried to buoy her up through her rough patches. They all heard the stories of how so many men had ended up ghosting her. It perplexed them all how supposedly nice men could disappoint their sweet friend. Ann didn't deserve such rotten treatment, and each and every friend of Ann's were pulling for her to find love once more. To lose her husband, then when she emerged from her grief and wanted to move on, it just wasn't fair how Ann couldn't catch a break in the romance department. It was the consensus of all that she deserved another man in her life.

By the time the ladies had dissected the drama of the evening and said their goodnights in the parking lot, it was after 11:30 when Ann finally pulled out from the Legion parking lot. She got home, got ready for bed quickly, and exhaustedly fell into bed. After tossing and turning for a while, thinking about Andy and what a great time she had, she finally fell asleep.

The phone rang, startling her awake. It was 1 a.m. Ann sat up in bed, knowing it could never be good news getting a call in the middle of the night.

"Is this Ann?" said a female voice, sounding very far away.

"Yes, this is Ann. What's wrong?" She felt panic rising.

"This is Heather at El Carrero Hospital, the hospital of Silicon Valley. You have a son, Connor?"

"Yes, yes! What's wrong?"

"We have Connor here in the emergency room. We are admitting him to ICU now. We found your contact info in his walle…."

Ann interrupted, frantic, "What's wrong? What happened? Is he okay? Tell me!!"

The woman continued to speak in a calm, soothing voice, explaining he had been in an accident, seemed to be stable, but it would be best if Ann could get there as soon as possible. Ann grabbed the pad of paper on her nightstand and a pencil, scribbling down the information she was given. She kept asking questions, not wanting to break communication with this person who was a lifeline to Connor. But after repeating all the information several times, the woman again urged Ann to arrive as soon as possible, and said goodbye.

Ann hung up the phone and jumped out of bed. She started for the bathroom, spun in a circle back to the phone. What should she do first? She was panicking. She took a deep breath, tried to think. She grabbed the phone again and dialed her next-door neighbor. As it rang, she felt bad disturbing her friend this late, but Debby answered on the second ring. Ann explained the whole story, her voice rising with panic, not knowing what to do or how to handle everything.

Debby instantly took charge. "Here's what will happen. I will arrange for your flight to San Jose and your car rental." Bless her heart, Ann thought, she remembered when Ann told her about when they had flown out there to get Connor settled in his apartment. "First thing you will do is go down to the kitchen and call me back with your credit card number. The airline won't want to use my card. Then you get dressed and pack a suitcase. By the time you are back downstairs in your kitchen, I'll bring over all the printouts of flight and rental info. Pick out a tote bag and put a few magazines and books in there. Get your phone off the charger and put it in your purse, along with the information the hospital lady gave you. I will drive you to the airport and drop you off. Everything is going to be fine. Now hang up and call me back when you have your credit card number."

It all unfolded exactly as Debby's soothing voice had explained. She even confirmed that Ann had complied with all the instructions. By the time they were in Debby's car heading for the airport, Ann was crying softly and her friend kept reassuring her that it was all going to be okay.

Ann tried to be strong on the flight out west. She had the puzzle book in her tote bag and tried to occupy herself with complicated word games, but her mind kept wandering back to Connor. She had just lost her husband; she couldn't lose her son too. She closed her eyes for a while, hoping to quiet her mind, and realized with a start that she must have slept almost the entire flight. The plane was beginning its descent and the ding of the plane intercom announced the landing instructions. Ann began gathering her sweater, tote bag and purse, and was ready to deplane as soon as they were allowed.

She joined the throng of passengers at the baggage claim, grateful that her bag was one of the first to come around the carrousel. She grabbed it, wheeled the bag out, and headed for the rental car area. She fished the paper Debby had printed out with the rental info on it and found the correct counter. Signatures, waiting for the shuttle, being delivered to her car, starting her drive. It was all very smooth and orderly, thank goodness. Debby had even printed out a sheet of directions from the airport to the hospital, and Ann consulted it now. Fifteen minutes away from her son.

Before the flight, Ann had called Debby from the gate as she was ready to board and had promised to call her again after she picked up her car. Stopped at a light, Ann reached into her purse, fumbling around for her phone. She couldn't feel it. When the light turned green, Ann pulled over into a gas station, stopped the car and dragged her purse onto her lap to find the phone. It still wasn't there. She began pulling everything out, and then, everything from her tote bag. And her pockets. And her sweater pockets. Her phone was gone. She opened the car door, got out, and leaned in, feeling all around the seat, between the upholstery and the seat, and under the floor mats. No phone.

She took a deep breath and talked to herself. This is not the most important thing right now. Get to the hospital and see Connor now. Deal with the phone later. She got back into the car, closed the door behind her, and pulled out to continue her drive to the hospital.

After leaving the rental car in the hospital parking lot, Ann entered the hospital and requested Connor's room number from the front desk, mentioning the family code she had received on the phone. She took the elevator to the third floor and walked quickly down the corridor. As she approached the correct room, she realized this was not intensive care. So this must be good news, if her son was in a regular room!

She knocked gently and entered. There was Connor, sitting up in his bed, clad in a standard hospital gown. He looked up and saw her.

"Hey, mom. What are you doing here?!?"

"What am I doing here??! What are YOU doing here???"

"Oh," he said casually, "I took a spill on my bike and sorta got run over. I'm fine."

"What?!? Run over? What happened?" She noticed now one of his arms was in a sling.

Connor started explaining. He and some of his friends from work were out for a bike ride, and they had crossed a patch of gravel. His friends had made it past, but he had spun out, fallen from his bike, and landed in the street just as a car was going by. The doctors told him he was unconscious for a few hours, they had set his broken arm, and he had just been transferred to this room.

Horrified, Ann asked if the car had hit him.

"We really don't know. My buddies were ahead of me, and nobody saw what happened. An ambulance took me here, and I don't remember anything. Hey, how did you know I was here?"

She backtracked and told her portion of the story. She asked whether he was wearing a helmet, if he was in pain now, and if there were any internal injuries. Connor answered what he could, and just then, his doctor entered the room.

As the physician examined her son, Ann looked at Connor, amazed that he appeared to be out of danger. Shining a light in his eyes, the expert asked him a few questions about his vision, headaches and nausea, felt along his hairline, then snapped off his gloves and turned to face Ann.

"You're the mom?" The doctor shook her hand and introduced himself. "We're all very lucky to still have this fine young man around now. We'll keep him a few more hours to check for signs of concussion, and we're awaiting the results of the MRI. If everything looks good this evening, Connor can go home."

Ann collapsed into the guest chair with relief. "I was so worried!"

The doctor backed out of the room, smiling, and a nurse came in to check Connor's dressings, pulling the gown down slightly. Now Ann could see gauze bandages, surgical tape and red patches on his skin. Oh my, he was lucky to be alive! She took a deep breath, let it out slowly, and said a silent prayer she still had her son.

When they were alone again, Connor started peppering his mom with questions, instructions for fetching his things from his apartment, and finally, expressing his remorse that she had to come all this way just for him. Ann lightly caressed his soft blonde hair, afraid to touch him but unable to not touch him. Connor looked so much like Pete, it was disconcerting. She hadn't seen him since he was home for his dad's funeral, and he had stuck around then for a few weeks. It was comforting to have him there, and his presence really helped as they tackled the snarl of red tape ever-present after someone dies suddenly. But she knew she couldn't keep him from his life, his job and his friends. It had been up to Ann to navigate her life without her husband, so she had encouraged Connor to get back to California. Now, she kissed his forehead, got out her notepad and started writing down his instructions.

Once Ann returned with Connor's phone charger, change of clothes, another pair of shoes, and specific grooming items he wanted, she felt ready to attack her next crisis. While Connor dozed, she used his phone to find phone numbers for the car rental counter, the airline gate back where she had first boarded, and the airport snack bar where she had purchased an apple, some nuts and a bottle of water. She then called all those places and gave the description of her phone. Nothing had been found. She was connected to the airline lost and found, and that didn't pan out either. She called Debby, who by now was frantic with worry since getting no further calls. Ann apologized profusely for causing her friend such distress and gave Debby an update on Connor and losing her phone.

Ann had tried calling her phone, but it went right to voicemail, so she still didn't know if it was lost or stolen, dead, or hacked and in use. She called her carrier, and was very angry at herself for not having installed a 'find my phone' app. She called her bank and credit card companies just in case and inquired with local law enforcement if they needed her to report the missing device. So many calls! Then she found the location of the nearest phone store and was pleased it was only five minutes from the hospital.

She waited for Connor to wake up, and after determining he didn't need anything more, she said she'd be back in a half hour; there was an errand she needed to run. She hadn't wanted to distress her son with her carelessness. She was already beating herself up enough for being so irresponsible to have lost her smartphone and she felt the withdrawal from being connected. Maybe it was irrational, but Ann felt helpless, powerless and vulnerable without her phone. It was not a good feeling.

At the phone store, she explained her predicament. The staff helped her pick out a new phone and asked her to enter her password to restore her apps. Luckily, she remembered it, so was hoping this whole nightmare would be behind her momentarily. But alas, not quite. It turns out, only her photos had been backed up to the cloud, so she lost her contacts, notes, messages and more. Ann remained cheerful, however, because Connor was going to be fine. And after all, family is what really counts.

159

It was closer to an hour by the time Ann returned to the hospital. She felt a bit guilty, knowing she could have missed the update from the physician, news of the test results, and discharge forecast. Again she berated herself for being so irresponsible to have lost her phone. SHE was supposed to be the one taking charge of Connor's situation, not acting as the victim.

And to add insult to injury, there were no available spots in the hospital parking garage this time, and Ann had to drive around and around, looking for somewhere to leave her car. Finally snagging a spot just as somebody was leaving, she practically ran the distance through the hospital lobby to the elevator and sprinted down the corridor to the room.

Where she found a surprise. A young blonde woman was sitting on the edge of Connor's bed, holding his hand. A purse slung over her shoulder. No aide or nurse's uniform. Hmmm.

"Hi, mom," Connor said. "Meet Anita, my girlfriend!"

"Well, hello!" said Ann, formally shaking the woman's hand. Everyone started talking at once. Apparently, Connor had never mentioned her to his mom before, because the relationship had been too new and tenuous. Anita was happy to meet her boyfriend's mother, knowing what an extraordinary background he had. And Ann was just very happy her son had found love.

They had been together over three months. Anita worked in the fitness center on Google's campus, and she had been helping Connor meet his fitness goals when they had started dating. Ann was able to draw her out a bit, and the young lady seemed intelligent, well-spoken, and was crazy about her son. They were both 25, shared similar interests, and in fact, Anita had been bike riding with him on the fateful spin-out episode that created this whole drama.

Ann sat in the guest chair, grinning at the happy turn of events. She learned that Anita was an 'only' as well, with no siblings, was learning to quilt from her grandmother, and she played a mean guitar. "So, how about that,"

Connor grinned at his mom. "You're Ann, she's Anita, and you're both musicians and quilters!"

The doctor came in just then and said the test results were in. There appeared to be no internal injuries or concussion, and the nurse would be in shortly with the discharge orders. Anita left because she had to get back to work, and Ann settled in to prepare for her son's release. While at Connor's apartment, she had remembered how, when setting up Connor's new place, she had insisted the sofa they would purchase had to open up into a bed for company. And now she would be sleeping in that bed. Imagine that!

She and Pete had visited Connor in California many times, but always during a scheduled seminar of Pete's, where they had been booked into a luxury hotel nearby. So now she was actually looking forward to sharing Connor's life for a few days while he recuperated. It would be a treat to act as caregiver for her 'baby' again.

The nurse arrived with the discharge information, including a follow-up appointment in ten days. Showering, driving and wound care instructions were all detailed on the folder of papers, and Ann accepted them gravely. Inside, she was grinning.

The rest of her visit flew by. Ann went grocery shopping and stocked her son's fridge, cooking for him and freezing many meals to help him out. She met lots of Connor's friends as they stopped by to see how their buddy had fared from the accident. He was able to work remotely from his laptop in a few days once the pain meds were no longer necessary. Finally reassured her son was doing great, Ann broached the subject of her leaving. Connor reacted with just the right amount of agreement without appearing eager to have her gone, so Ann booked her return flight.

"Onward and upward," Ann pronounced as she finally hugged Connor goodbye, holding him a bit too long. She realized she didn't know when she'd see him next.

To: Betty <MommyOfAnn>
From: Ann <QuiltingFanatic>
Date: today

Thank you for being so supportive, mom, while I was in California. Talking to you every day really kept my spirits up. Connor is such a joy....I'm very proud of the man he has become. I wish Pete could see him now. Do you and dad still plan on swinging by there when you're in San Francisco next month? Include a weekday and ask him for the Google tour...it will boggle your mind!

I'm back to my regular routine of quilting, guild meetings, ukulele practicing and jam sessions, storytelling gigs, line dancing and volunteering. Luckily, I hadn't had to miss any speaking engagements while visiting Connor. I don't have any subs I can call to have them cover for me in a crisis...I should probably find some.

The problem is, most speakers I run across use so many fillers, it drives me crazy. For example: um, like, you know, er. Once, a speaker at my quilt guild, supposedly a professional, said 'you know' so many times, I started counting. By the end of her speech, she had said it 48 times! I truly believe a respectable speaker owes their audience a presentation without dysfluencies. Yes, I'm 'preaching to the choir', aren't I?! I remember when I was a teen, you broke me of the habit of using 'like' so often! So, thanks, mom!!

The whole cell phone fiasco is still dogging me, as I keep discovering more and more things I lost. Apps I forgot I don't have any more. Reminder notes I've lost. Having to recreate my Contacts list is a pain in the butt. And I've lost a new friend's phone number that I really wanted and can't replace it. Oh, well, it's always something.

When I think how close I came to losing Connor, I really freak out. If that car had been just six inches further over....I don't even want to think about it! I've been checking on him every day since I left, and I think he's starting to feel smothered. I know I have to back off, but it's hard. I have really high hopes for this Anita that he's dating….I really like her…how can I not, she's a quilter! Hopefully you'll meet her next month; you'll have to tell me what you think of her! Be sure to study Connor's face when he looks at her, and it will give you all the insight you need….

Oh, on a slightly unrelated topic, remember back when I told you the story of the night he was born? Of course, you don't, it was 25 years ago! But in my quite memorable birth story from that night, I was awakened by somebody screaming, and I was in advanced labor. So now, the oddest thing happened to me one of the nights I was sleeping in Connor's apartment. I woke up at 3 am; it must have been a bad dream. And it suddenly hit me, after all these years. It was ME screaming that night. My labor started again and woke me up, and it must have been an involuntary shriek. Pete hadn't been in the room at that exact moment, so he couldn't confirm it. I wish he were here, so I could tell him my theory!

I've been watching the weather reports in the Florida area near you, and hoping no violent storms affect you.

Anyway, talk to you soon.

Love,
Ann

A disadvantage of living in a heavily wooded neighborhood in autumn is that it has so many trees. The same quality that provides such beauty and shade in the spring and summer. But as the weather cools and the green leaves turn to shades of orange, yellow and brown, the attractiveness of the area turns into a massive autumn chore. Raking. But Pete didn't mind.

There were twelve large trees on their property when they had purchased it, but over the years, they had lost a few. One giant oak tree was struck by lightning during a storm; the huge boom had shaken the house. Pieces of bark flew one hundred feet, damaging the siding on theirs and several neighboring houses, but luckily, no fire or major structural damage had occurred. Then gradually, several trees had aged out, weakening and dying. It was sad to have to hire a company to come remove them, but it was safer to take them down than to have them fall.

Pete loved trees. Always had. He wasn't a tree-hugging hippie kind of guy, but he appreciated their majestic beauty. As well, he saw their value in keeping the house cooler in the summer from their natural shade. He oversaw maintaining their health by hiring companies that handled trimming, spraying, and cabling branches when necessary. In fact, if a neighbor was having a large tree cut down and Pete noticed the huge trucks arriving, he would watch the proceedings. He'd settle in by the living room picture window in the upholstered rocker that could swivel, and he'd oversee the goings-on, rotating his chair as necessary to scrutinize the laborers as they worked. Ann always found it amazing that he could watch the action for as long as it took.

The community where they lived had a leaf collection schedule. Residents were to rake their leaves onto the edge of the street, on their tree lawn by the sidewalk. The large vacuuming trucks would rumble down the street, with one employee driving, one raking the leaves into the path, and one swinging the giant vacuuming hose to suck them up. Not surprisingly, Pete enjoyed watching this task if he happened to be around when he heard the truck come down their street.

When the leaves started falling, he enjoyed collecting them with his lawn mower. He would empty the collection bag along the tree lawn, lengthening the piles to wrap around their corner lot. When there were too many leaves for the mower to handle, he'd use a leaf blower. The high-pitched whine of blowers would reverberate through the neighborhood as home owners kept up with this chore. And then there was good old-fashioned raking, and Pete was always on the lookout for the newest designs and technology in rakes at the home stores. Ann would laugh when he'd bring home a new rake, asking why he needed a new one when they already owned so many. He'd smile happily and point out the features of what he'd purchased, how it would be so much more efficient.

And so today was a raking day. The city crew had been down their street a week earlier, so Pete knew he had a few more days until their return trip. He wanted to get the last of the leaves ready for pickup, taking advantage of the unusually mild November weather. After lunch, he had donned his old red flannel shirt and a grubby pair of blue jeans. His battered work boots and beige work gloves completed the ensemble. He had kissed Ann as he went out the door through the garage to tackle the task.

An hour later, Ann had just finished gathering up the Halloween accessories when she heard Pete burst in from the garage. He was shrieking incoherently about the most horrible headache, and he wanted to go the hospital NOW. This was so scary on so many levels…Pete never raised his voice, ever. He hated doctors and hospitals and could hardly be convinced to go. And as he grabbed his jacket off the hook, he made his way to the passenger side of Ann's car, waiting for her to drive him…he always wanted to be the driver. Ann was alarmed, scared and panicked.

She grabbed her purse and keys, and tried to be reassuring. She would get him over there in five minutes, she said. Everything would be fine, she said. The doctors would help him, she insisted. Pete kept shouting with the pain and panic, telling her to go through red lights and just get him there quickly.

Everything happened in a blur. Ann pulled up to the emergency entrance, threw the car into park and jumped out to get help, but Pete had thrown the

165

car door open and was running towards the entrance, screaming. People were turning to look as the two of them burst into the registration area. Staff were at their side immediately, and Pete continued to scream and moan, holding his head, as they wheeled him through the double doors.

Ann hurriedly surrendered her insurance card, answered the most necessary questions, and was told to go park her car in the lot. She did so quickly, numb from shock, and then was led back to the triage area. Pete was laying on a bed, silent, an IV inserted, and his eyes were closed. She was told they had given him pain medication, he was going for a CT scan now, and the surgeon would be in to speak with her.

As they wheeled Pete out for the test, a nurse put her hand on Ann's arm. "Honey, do you have a friend or family member who can come sit with you?"

Ann stared at her. "Why, is he going to die?"

"Just call somebody to be with you, dear," she repeated, and walked out of the cubicle. Ann grabbed her phone from her purse, and was just debating who would be available to rush over here right that minute when a white-coated doctor came in.

He introduced himself, gravely shook her hand, and instantly began a rush of doctor-speak about burst brain aneurysms, what they were and how they were treated. She could barely follow when he started talking about endovascular coiling, artery catheters and chances of survival. She slipped her phone back into her purse and started to fumble around for a pad of paper and a pen to take notes, when Pete was wheeled back in.

He was ashen, his eyes were half open, and she rushed to him, cradling his head. Instinctively, she knew what was happening, and sobbing, Ann held Pete as he died.

Staff had left the room to give her privacy, and time seemed to stand still for Ann. Eventually, things were going on around her, with nurses entering, machines being wheeled out, sounds that seemed to come from far away. She felt like she was floating above the bed, looking down from the ceiling, watching the activity in the room. It couldn't be her 45-year-old husband who had just died. That was too young. He was too healthy. It was too quick.

Eventually, she straightened up, pulled a tissue from a box on the counter, wiped her eyes, blew her nose, and tossed the used tissue in the trash can. She had many questions now. She looked from face to face seeking the best person to ask.

Then the doctor who had introduced himself came back in, indicated she should follow him to his office down the hall. Ann looked back at Pete on the bed, hesitant to leave him. But she obeyed, knowing she could ask her questions. They walked quickly down the corridor and entered a sterile looking office. The doctor indicated she should sit, then he sat behind his desk, and he began explaining.

"Your husband had an aneurysmal subarachnoid hemorrhage, SAH. Approximately 15% of patients with SAH die before reaching the hospital. Most of the deaths from subarachnoid hemorrhage are due to rapid and massive brain injury from the initial bleeding which is not correctable by medical and surgical interventions."

He stopped and studied her carefully. "Are you still with me?"

"Yes, I understand, doctor. But he was only 45!"

"Actually," he continued, "brain aneurysms are most prevalent in people ages 35 to 60. I know this won't make you feel any better, but there are almost half a million deaths worldwide each year caused by brain aneurysms and half the victims are younger than 50."

"You're right, it's not much comfort. But thank you for explaining."

"And another thing," the doctor said, "over half the people who recover from a ruptured brain aneurysm will have disabilities, such as vision deficits or complete blindness, speech or memory difficulties, ambulation issues, and more. I just wanted you to know this."

"But could we have had advance warning this thing in his brain was about to burst?" Ann asked.

"Unruptured brain aneurysms are typically completely asymptomatic. Meaning, the patient shows no symptoms whatsoever. These aneurysms are typically small in size, usually less than one half inch in diameter. Your husband's first symptom was the worst headache of his life, am I correct?" Ann nodded. "Then, no, he had no earlier symptoms, most likely. He could have had blurred or double vision, weakness or numbness, or had difficulty speaking. Did he exhibit any of these prior to your bringing him here?"

"I don't think so," Ann said thoughtfully. "He would have said something, I would think."

"Yes," the doctor continued. "I would imagine. In his circumstances, there was absolutely nothing we could have done. Nothing more YOU could have done. I want you to remember that."

BLOG: Therefore I Quilt

Quilting Goals?

Posted: Dec 27, 2018 08:15 AM EST

As the new year approaches, many people make resolutions. These are so easy to break, so maybe as quilters, we should just think about what we could improve in 2018.

Do you resolve to make a sample block first before you cut out the whole quilt, and avoid possible disaster? Or put things away where they belong in your sewing space so you can find them again? Shop in your own stash before buying more? Or buy that notion you really want but have been putting off...your local quilt shop can probably get it for you!

Maybe you feel compelled to finish some long-forgotten projects. Or reversely, drop the guilt, donate them away and move on! Perhaps you need to shake things up in the new year. Join a quilt guild. Make/donate your first charity quilt. Drop those feed dogs and free motion quilt. Try a technique you never tried before: paper piecing, set-in seams, applique, mitered borders, curved piecing, etc. Perhaps time management is your goal...consider setting aside ten or twenty minutes every day to sew.

Or sew something new to YOU: a miniature, a bed-sized quilt, a purse or placemats...there are endless choices. Ask around for suggestions to shake up your creativity in 2018...the sky's the limit!

Comment on this blog what YOU resolve—no pressure, though!   ~Ann

169

Ann cleared an entire day to spend sewing in her studio. She really wanted to catch up on those projects with deadlines. She had been thinking a lot about what she had posted on her most recent blog entry. Making resolutions, planning how to improve. It seemed like her life could use a thorough revamp. This last year, she had really opened herself up to finding love again, and nothing had worked out. It had been a roller coaster of high hopes and crushing let-downs. She felt like she was in a romantic comedy that had gone wrong. But if this were a movie, a final scene would have shown the heroine meeting a Prince Charming who swept her off her feet, and they would live happily ever after. Ann didn't think real life worked like that.

She sat at her sewing machine, ready to sew the borders on her architectural quilt top that had been waiting for almost a year. Now she had promised this quilt to the local home remodelers' group annual meeting as a raffle prize to raise money for a local charity. The deep blue border would nicely set off the center piecing. Ann had planned it to end up a large throw-sized quilt, perfect for cuddling under on the sofa, for the lucky winner. The event was in six weeks, so she had to finish the top, create a fabric backing, and layer the whole thing on her ping pong table sandwiched with the batting. Then she would quilt it in a large meander stitch, trim and bind it, and add a personalized label with washing instructions. When it was done, she would meet her contact person at the nearby coffee shop to deliver the quilt, and he would be thrilled his group was the recipient of such a valuable textile gift.

The border was pinned in place, the sewing machine turned on, and Ann was ready. But she just sat there staring out the window. What was wrong with her? She had put herself out there multiple times, and each time it hadn't worked out. Yeah, she admitted to herself, she went to the wrong coffee shop and blew it right out of the gate, but what about all the rest? She started counting on her fingers: four different times, she had considered a nice man, but he had dropped off the face of the earth. Or someone she thought had potential turned out to be married. Or gay. Or an alcoholic. Or never showed up for their meeting. One guy only wanted to list her house, and another one she can't contact, even though she wanted to. And turning into a lesbian wasn't a solution, either! Heck, she couldn't even give away Pete's workshop tools....what was WRONG with her?!?

Ann turned off her sewing machine and put the quilt top back on her table. No quilting right this minute; it was time for a pity party. She stood up. She looked around. Was this the right location for feeling sorry for herself? She was a 45-year-old woman, her husband had died way too young, and even though she felt ready to let another man into her life, the perfect man obviously was not out there.

Ann walked out of her studio and went into the guest room down the hall. She closed the door and stood before the full-length mirror on the back, studying her reflection. Now that she was slender and wearing fashionable clothes that fit her well, she thought men would find her desirable. A decent enough face, brown hair with no gray she could see, and people have commented many times that her color flecked brown eyes were beautiful.

Maybe there is just one soulmate per person in this world, and Pete was hers. But geez, no man even wanted to ask her out? Was there something wrong with her? She admitted to herself that she made herself available all the time, considering all her activities. She felt confident, was a decent conversationalist, and was warm and welcoming to others. She mingled with lots of men all the time and thought they would have ample opportunities to consider her as a special friend. At the hospital, her Fat Busters meetings, line dancing, the grief group, fundraisers, ukulele jam sessions, her storytelling, online dating, euchre group, singles group....how much MORE could she get herself out there?! Obviously, this was not meant to be.

She sighed, opened the door and walked back to her studio. She sat back down at her sewing machine, picked up the quilt top and turned on the sewing machine again. She found where the first seam would begin, raised the presser foot, inserted the fabric, removed the first pin, and was ready to press on the foot pedal.

And right then, a spider dropped from the ceiling, right onto the edge of her sewing table. A big, brown, ugly, scary spider. Directly in front of her, about six inches from her face. Ann sharply inhaled, reached over to the table and grabbed a tissue from the box. She crumpled the tissue and jammed it down over the spider, squished it between the layers and tossed the carnage into the wastebasket. She realized she was holding her breath and let it out slowly.

She stood up. Oh. My. Goodness. She had just killed a spider. By herself. A really huge one. She doesn't need a man to kill her spiders. She can do it all alone! She turned off her sewing machine again and grabbed her phone.

Elaine, you available?

Yeah, I'm here. What's up?

I just had an epiphany.
Wanted to share. I realized I
don't need another man. I'm
completely fine the way
things are. I have a full life,
wonderful girlfriends, my
activities are enjoyable, I'm
financially secure, my son
has a serious girlfriend,
someday I could have
grandchildren. Life is good.

Yay for you, Ann!

Yeah. Pete was my
soulmate, and there will
never be another Pete. We're
only dancing on this earth for
a short while, and I thank you
for being here with me. But
now I have to get back to my
latest quilt. Onward and
upward!

173

Acknowledgements

I owe many thanks to my three sons, Evan, Eric and Ross. My whining emails to them requesting technical assistance on business details were usually met with good natured suggestions. Or else they ignored me. In both cases, it was helpful.

Additional thanks to Evan for helping me plan the covers of this book. The mosaic quilt I had designed and sewn almost seven years ago looks better with the purple color wash than it does in person!

National Novel Writing Month (www.nanowrimo.org) provided the impetus for me to become a real author. I write Facebook posts, quilting newsletter articles, and blog posts for my favorite quilt shop. But never before have I written a novel. I usually read nonfiction, not fiction. So to write a novel when I don't usually read them is sorta ironic. Having to produce 50,000 words in 30 days is indeed a challenge.

I credit my sister Eileen for her request that I be her writing buddy during this wild ride. She lit the fire under me, made invaluable suggestions, and encouraged me to write this novel. My niece Melanie was helpful also.

Many friends were supportive to me on this journey. Thank you to Hattie Kate for her suggestion to "show, don't tell," Sharon for her confidence in me, Greg for his technical advice, and Patty and Janis for their enthusiasm. My Facebook friends offered suggestions as well, and I appreciate their input. Thank you to my fellow participants in Get Fit and Frog Ladies, who waited anxiously to read my work. And thanks to Cathy of my local quilt shop for allowing me to include here some blog posts I had written for them.

Thank you to the internet for the answers to my many questions in my book prep work, such as: What nicknames are there for overweight people? Do you resign college at the registrar or bursar? What happens immediately after a baby is born? What are the most fattening foods? How many different foot problems are there? What's the name for the razor blade tool you use for crafts? Whether the answers I found are accurate or not, who knows?!

Special thanks to my long-suffering husband, Donald. Here's an example: Knowing I would be extremely busy during National Novel Writing Month, I was hesitant to request some library books I wanted. I asked him, "If my books have to be picked up this month, will you go get them for me?" He replied, "Maybe. Will you be nice to me?" I responded, "No, I will be a bitch the whole month from nerves." He gave me a dirty look for swearing. I so appreciate Don's help in meal prep, house cleaning, lawn care and bill paying while I frantically wrote this novel. No, wait, I appreciate his handling these things ALL the time. This guy's a keeper. Thanks, sweetie.

About the Author

Sheila Painter is a storyteller, active volunteer, and award-winning quilter. She also enjoys jigsaw and crossword puzzles. She lives in the Toledo, Ohio area, is married to Donald Painter, has three sons and five grandchildren.

Made in the USA
Monee, IL
04 April 2022